Don Morris

KATHERINE FAW is the author of *Ultraluminous*, an Indie Next pick, which was named a best book of the year by *The New Yorker*, *BOMB*, and Vulture. Her debut novel, *Young God*, was long-listed for the Center for Fiction First Novel Prize and named a best book of the year by *The Times Literary Supplement*, the *Houston Chronicle*, BuzzFeed, and more. She was born in North Carolina. She lives in Brooklyn.

ALSO BY KATHERINE FAW

Young God

ULTRALUMINOUS

ULTRALUMINOUS

KATHERINE FAW

PICADOR   MCD   FARRAR, STRAUS AND GIROUX   NEW YORK

ULTRALUMINOUS. Copyright © 2017 by Katherine Faw. All rights reserved. Printed in the United States of America. For information, address Picador, 175 Fifth Avenue, New York, N.Y. 10010.

picadorusa.com • instagram.com/picador
twitter.com/picadorusa • facebook.com/picadorusa

Picador® is a U.S. registered trademark and is used by Macmillan Publishing Group, LLC, under license from Pan Books Limited.

For book club information, please visit facebook.com/picadorbookclub or email marketing@picadorusa.com.

Designed by Abby Kagan

The Library of Congress has cataloged the MCD edition as follows:

Names: Morris, Katherine Faw, 1983– author.
Title: Ultraluminous / Katherine Faw.
Description: First edition. | New York: Farrar, Straus and Giroux, 2017.
Identifiers: LCCN 2017024483 | ISBN 9780374279660 (hardcover) | ISBN 9780374716646 (ebook)
Subjects: LCSH: Prostitutes—Fiction. | Terrorists—Fiction. | GSAFD: Suspense fiction.
Classification: LCC PS3613.O7733 U47 2017 | DDC 813'.6—dc23
LC record available at https://lccn.loc.gov/2017024483

Picador Paperback ISBN 978-1-250-19273-8

Our books may be purchased in bulk for promotional, educational, or business use. Please contact your local bookseller or the Macmillan Corporate and Premium Sales Department at 1-800-221-7945, extension 5442, or by email at MacmillanSpecialMarkets@macmillan.com.

First published by MCD, an imprint of Farrar, Straus and Giroux

First Picador Edition: December 2018

For You, Love Me

ULTRALUMINOUS

/

I met a man, when I was a whore in Dubai, who shook my hand and then passed it to his other palm and held it there. At the time it was mildly confusing. Now I know what he was doing. He was trying to see if I was wide-open, if he could fill my mind with anything.

I am cold and naked except for a G-string and money rubber-banded around my ankle. We are in a private room and already I took off my shoes. I put my hands on the soft wall to frame either side of his face. I bite my lip and then I look at him. I am back in New York so I can ask right away.

"What do you do?" I say.

2

On Broadway and Twenty-Eighth I stand in the middle of a bike lane. I look at a bike coming at me. A woman rings her bell furiously. She has a basket on her bike. She's wearing a helmet.

"Get out of the bike lane," she screams.

I don't.

"Get out of the bike lane."

The bell rings louder and louder and her eyes, nose, and lips pucker more and more toward the center of her face.

"Are you fucking deaf?" she says.

She swerves. New York is different.

On the menu are all the stomachs of the cow, first through fourth. This guy orders the calf's brain special.

"Excellent," the waiter says.

"Are you a zombie?" I say to the guy.

The guy laughs.

"Are you a peasant?"

"What?" the guy says.

"Are you afraid you might die from lack of protein?"

"It's a delicacy."

"That's what you want me to think."

I hand the waiter the menu.

"I'll have the tongue sampler," I say.

After the waiter is gone the guy scowls at me.

"I should burn your hand."

Set into the table between us is an electric grill.

"God, I was just joking," I say.

I get off the L train and go into a bodega. The floor looks new. I examine it.

"So this is Brooklyn?"

"Yeah," the bodega guy says.

"You don't have to put down cardboard when it rains?"

"We have rugs," he says.

They stunned me at first, the towers on the Williamsburg waterfront. They're a growth of glass with crooked-looking balconies. This guy's in one of them. On his balcony he has long-haired AstroTurf.

"It's the closest you can get to real grass. It took me six months to find it."

"Do you worry this balcony will fall off?"

"No," he says.

I sit on the railing and lean back into Manhattan. The guy grabs a lawn chair like he's catching me.

"Let's go inside," he says.

His kitchen is shiny chrome. He has a quartz island. This apartment looks like a show apartment. It's like he doesn't live here at all except for his coke. He puts his computer in front of me.

"Just hit the space bar to flip through."

"Is that you?"

"Yeah. That's in Cuba. Before everybody could go there. That beard is real hair," he says.

He's also wearing the Castro cap. In the photo he's fucking a Cuban girl from behind on a motel bed.

"You're a photographer?" I say.

"They're stills from video. I'm an artist."

He's a banker. I bend over to do a line. His lines are short and thin.

"Political art is the worst," I say.

His laugh is short, too.

I wander into this bar in the morning.

"Surprise me," I say to the bartender.

On the bar he puts a plastic cup inset with a plastic shot glass. He pours cherry vodka in the center. He cracks a Red Bull and dumps it over the top.

"Cherry Bomb."

"Gross," I say.

It tastes like Robitussin. The others are watching me. I'm the only one in here who isn't the color gray. I light a cigarette and look at the bartender.

"Am I breaking the law?"

"This is a cop bar," the bartender says.

I slide my pack to him. He lights one for himself.

Every girl at the gym has a tattoo but very few have fake boobs. The girl beside me has a big circle on her back. In the middle it says TODAY. It looks drawn by a child or mental patient. I wait until we both turn off our hair dryers.

"When you die everybody will know it's you."

"What?" she says.

I look at her back. In the locker room mirror she looks at us.

"That's good," she says.

I collect my empty heroin bags. They are stamped, which is a thing I have missed. The stamp on this brick is LV. As in Louis Vuitton but without the checker pattern, just floating. There is a right way to do heroin and that is with a structure. I'm not supposed to be saving anything.

———

I left in Dubai a closet of beautiful dresses. They were every color and fabric. It gave me a shot of pleasure to open the door and see the seductive pattern they made out of chaos.

On Sixth Avenue I stop on the street to look at a dusty Polish fashion magazine from the 1990s. It is priced at two hundred thousand zlotys.

"Just two hundred thousand?" I say.

The man selling it looks up from under his hood and I see that his nose is grotesque in every way. It's long, twisted, bulbous, and pitted. I suddenly feel like I'm not in America, where no one has a nose like this. I wait for what he's going to say like he has a message for me.

"Five dollars," he says.

"Here we have checks on hyperinflation," I say.

"For you four dollars," he says.

This guy wants to buy me something. We go to Barneys. I am disconcerted that no one offers me coffee and dates. Behind a rack of see-through shirts he sticks his hand up my skirt.

"Shopping makes you wet," he says.

"I'm always wet," I say.

I try on a pair of red velvet and also gilded Mary Jane stiletto pumps that look like teacups. I turn a little circle in front of the foot mirror.

"Now I can't run away from you."

"Exactly," he says.

In the brushed metal of the elevator I am much taller than him now.

"Kata?"

I forget this is my name.

"Yes, baby," I say.

———

I'm back in Brooklyn. I can look up and see the art guy's apartment but I'm not with him. Under a pink tent with a top that appears blood-splattered a girl is selling anarchy-branded jam.

"Are you an anarchist?"

The girl looks at me from behind a table.

"I just work here," she says.

"Are the people who make this anarchists?"

"I don't think so."

"Like sometimes they piss in the jars?"

"Definitely not."

She laughs.

"Anarchists wouldn't do that," she says.

I pick a spicy orange marmalade.

"How much, then?"

The tents are pitched on a slab of concrete that's roped in. They all have aesthetic logos. The fumes from their gas stoves are nauseating. Everything looks clever and smells flammable. This guy is crouched at the end of a crowded picnic table. He has a fried fish sandwich dripping with coleslaw. He has what appears to be beer but is cold coffee.

"Tell me about yourself," he says.

"No," I say.

"You look Russian."

In Dubai that statement was a question: "Can I buy you?" I swallow a spoonful of jelly.

"I'm not Russian."

"You want some bread?"

He's old enough. He was a junk-bond trader in the 1980s. I really look at him for a second, as much as I can because we're both wearing sunglasses.

"Remember when eating was just a thing you did, not a thing?"

He shrugs. I stab the spoon in my jelly.

"Shit was twelve dollars," I say.

I danced for one week in three freezing strip clubs. My one requirement to make a date was that he have a good job in finance. When a man grabbed the back of my arm I had to turn around and smile. It didn't matter who smiled back. I move out of a hotel and into an apartment.

3

"I want to crawl on my hands and knees until I get to your feet and then I want to look up and ask you to please fuck me," I text to CBG.

New York wants to trick me, make me think it's gone soft. When I slide out of my high mules, on my feet are four stripes of grime.

The doorman at this club later is a midget. I look at the calf's brain guy in a weary way.

"What? This place is supposed to be hot," the calf's brain guy says.

I don't snicker with the doorman.

I gallery-hop with the art guy. We don't see any stills of artists dressed like dictators from faux-porn videos.

"All this shit sucks," I say.

"No, it doesn't," he says.

He seems agitated. In the biggest and whitest gallery in Chelsea we stare at ourselves in a gray mirror. Like any mirror, it rationally reflects what steps in front of it. I step to the side.

"I like this," I say.

I point.

"The blank wall?" the art guy says.

"It's the best thing we've seen all day."

The cop bar is locked. But I knock on the door and they buzz me in.

"Cherry Bomb," I say.

The bartender throws the empty Red Bull at the trash and misses it.

"That shit'll kill you."

I look at this guy two stools down. He's young, too. He's wearing a bad suit.

"That would make it easier," I say.

He nods at his beer.

"What's the most fucked-up thing you've ever seen?" I say.

Now I'm sitting on the stool next to him.

"At this club in Bogotá I bought some coke off this girl. It turned out she was a prostitute. Anyway, later I was following her, like down all these alleys, and out of nowhere the Colombian cops run up on us. They're yelling. They got guns. I got an eightball in my sock, you know, my whole fucking face is numb. So this chick pulls out a knife, slashes both her arms, and starts flinging her blood at the cops. She's screaming, 'AIDS, AIDS, AIDS,' and me and the cops are like, 'Holy fucking shit.' And then she said run and I did and they didn't follow us," he says.

I drink my Cherry Bomb.

"That's fucked-up," I say.

I feel a familiar happiness. I wait for it to go away.

There is a planet where it rains blue glass in 4,350-mile-per-hour winds. It rotates around a star that is not our sun. The Sheikh told me that, one afternoon when we were naked, and I remember closing my eyes and trying to see it and laughing.

I give my hands to a girl who is supposed to be special, a pro in from Kyoto for two weeks only.

"I want my nails to look like galaxies," I say.

These new Duane Reades confuse me. They have their own granola mixes. They're wide-aisled and well lit. I wander through one aimlessly. I squat down in front of the moisturizers. On the bottom shelf are zero off-brand tubs of cocoa butter covered in dust. Near the registers is a refrigerated display of sushi rolls. I am incredulous. I buy the spicy tuna.

I unwrap the brick and it's stamped RPG. I stare at the delivery guy.

"RPG?"

"Shit's fire," he says.

I shut the door in his face.

At Opening Ceremony I try on a tank top and leggings with a matching print like a pajama set. The design is wolves' heads endlessly. The guy who buys me things shakes his head.

"I don't like that. It's tacky," he says.

"I want this," I say.

"Awesome," the salesgirl says.

The junk-bond guy takes me to the movies. We sit in the back row. As soon as the lights go down I give him a hand job. He tips his head into the black wall and grins. At the last second I put my head down and catch his come.

I watch a Romanian movie where nothing happens for probably two hours. Then the guy starts shooting people with a rifle.

4

A man shakes up a bottle of champagne and fizzes it over a girl's tilted-up face. The calf's brain guy and I are sitting on top of a couch.

"Everywhere you take me is so douchey," I say.

This club is thudding. It looks like a bunker.

"What?" he says.

I yell in his ear.

"Douchey."

This club has a stage show. On stage a naked guy is pulling condoms out of his ass and throwing them at the audience.

"Shit's crazy," the art guy says.

I roll my eyes. We're sitting at assigned tables. Our coat-check tickets are in my purse.

"Everyone's so professional like you," I say.

I turn around to see the naked guy behind me, just as he's dropping one of his condoms down the back of my dress. I jump like it's a live animal.

"Fuck," I say.

The art guy is laughing hard.

———

"I did four tours in Afghanistan."

I turn around on my stool until our knees knock.

"That makes sense," I say.

"Why?"

"Because of your face."

"My face?"

The guy in the cop bar scratches his cheek. I wave at the bartender.

"Another Cherry Bomb."

I don't charge the ex–Army Ranger in the ladies' bathroom of the cop bar. He sits on the closed toilet seat and I bounce up and down on his cock. He laughs. He buries his face in me.

Alone at home I snort an RPG bag and then I lick it. I have this water stain on my ceiling. It's curling and brown. I sit on my couch and in my mind I rip it out. I replaster and repaint, again and again. It never stays fixed. Sometimes it expands. I did notice it before I rented the apartment.

Near my apartment is a place that is just juice. It's all refrigerators. There are bottles in every color. They make a muted rainbow.

"Which one's the thickest?"

"The thickest?"

"Yeah," I say.

"I mean, the coconut milk's really filling," the cashier says.

I open the refrigerator and pull out three white bottles to coat my throat because heroin drip is disgusting. He smiles at me.

"Are you doing a cleanse?"

"Yes," I say.

I get my pussy waxed by a Brazilian lady all in white. She can tell I'm a whore. It's the tiniest smirk.

14

"Cute piercing," she says.

"Thanks," I say.

The dancer with the bigger tits has a little rip in her fishnets. It's an irritating flaw. I see it in the space between every strobe. She's not topless but she's getting paid enough to keep her stockings new. Fog cannons boom. The guy who buys me things pulls rosé from an ice bucket. When confetti drops from the ceiling the girls onstage open black umbrellas.

"That is such bad luck," I say.

"I don't believe in bad luck," he says.

"That's because you've always had good luck."

"I believe in reason."

I step down from the chair I'm standing on without explanation. I go outside to smoke and the sun squints my eyes shut.

All his molars are gold. I ask him to open his mouth wide.

"I thought I was the customer," the junk-bond guy says.

I run my tongue on them. He runs his finger up my arm.

"What's this?"

"Probably glitter," I say.

If I stay alive long enough, even though I do heroin right, a few at a time my teeth will snap off in my dry mouth.

"If mine fell out I'd get gold everywhere but I'll be dead by then."

He pulls down my bottom lip with his thumb.

"That's what everybody thinks," he says.

Once I was dumb. I would walk into a slippery restaurant on the arm of a slippery man in slippery clothes he had bought for me, and feel what he must have felt, like it was mine, and that was the feeling of victory.

———

I put on an outfit that is head-to-toe leopard-print. Sometimes I wear snakeskin instead. I walk around the block to the Polish diner and sit at a table by myself. I keep looking at the woman behind the register. She's been there all my life. Her eye shadow is as blue and thick as always. The waitress says something in Polish.

"I'm not Polish," I say.

"You look beautiful."

I look at her. I've never seen her before. She must have started sometime in the last decade and I don't care what she thinks of me. I shove the menu away.

"Pierogi. All cheese," I say.

5

The stamp's VERSACE, not floating this time but with the rest of the logo's design, which is the Medusa's head.

"This is much more sensible," I say.

"Can I have my money?" the delivery guy says.

I give it to him. I shut the door in his face.

"Tell me a story," the Sheikh said.

"In New York the heroin comes in bags with stamps that are pictures or words, like a bomb or BOOM, like a brand," I said.

"Like for children," he said.

The calf's brain guy is telling me about the famous chef. I'm not paying attention. This restaurant is claustrophobic. There are ten of us at a bar and the famous chef is behind it wearing a spotless suit. There's no menu. We get what he makes us and that's it. I feel the woman beside me is listening attentively to everything I say.

"This is like a dinner party you have to pay for," I say.

"Okay, you can pay for it," the calf's brain guy says.

I smirk at him. The famous chef slides white saucers in front of us, each with a single scarlet wafer. Then he steps back and tucks his hands in his vest.

"I snorted a bag of heroin before I came here so I don't really have an appetite," I say.

Then I laugh. The famous chef laughs, too. So does the woman beside me. I put the red wafer on my tongue.

"Dehydrated pig's blood," the famous chef says.

The calf's brain guy forces a finger between two of my ribs. I swallow it.

"Metallic," I say.

A feeling of illness lingers.

The art guy takes me to an exhibit of erotic nudes. I stare at a girl with her hands between her legs. She is skinnier than the rest, sallow and cat-faced, and just sketched, like she could be erased.

"You can tell by the look of contempt on their faces that these women are prostitutes," I say.

He looks at me.

"I read it on the wall."

"Mine too," the art guy says.

"What?"

I slide my fingers inside his cuffs.

"All of my models are prostitutes," he says.

There's a knock on the door. The ex-Ranger gets buzzed in.

"Good morning," I say.

He orders a beer but he says nothing. It's six a.m. We watch the weather on one of the cop bar's TVs.

"Who was that guy?"

"Who?" I say.

"The one you were with."

"Are you stalking me?"

The ex-Ranger drinks his beer. My tongue tastes like all the chemicals of a Cherry Bomb. I will give him the chance not to start this with me.

"Sometimes he pays my rent."

I look at him. He doesn't look at me. He nods.

A kid does a backflip on the overhead poles and almost smacks a woman in the face. I'm on the subway. This makes me feel better.

On my phone I scroll through the pictures of my ass. I text an anatomical one to GBT.

The guy who buys me things tongs a snow crab onto my plate. The grand seafood platter is always three tiers. Not until we pull all the flesh from all the shells will we get to leave.

"I used to want everything and now I don't want anything," I say.

He snorts like he doesn't believe me. I don't know if I believe me.

"You know how to crack that?" he says.

I summon something deeper than contempt. I pick up the crab by a pincher.

"Can you show me?"

He is instantly pleased.

I ask the counter guy for Russian dressing.

"You're from New York," the junk-bond guy says.

"So?" I say.

The pastrami is the same. I look around for the ex-Ranger but I don't find him.

Cigarettes are fourteen dollars and it's hard to get over it.

6

I get a lobster roll from a truck. I sit beside a street kid near the horse statue in Union Square. He looks at me.

"I'm sorry to bother you but could you possibly spare ten dollars?" he says.

"I read in *The New York Times* a bag of dope's only six dollars now," I say.

He looks like he might laugh. I cross my wolf legs Indian-style and bring the lobster up to my mouth.

"Cunt."

He gets up.

I meet the calf's brain guy at a chartreuse bar on the Lower East Side with a bouncer outside. A waitress brings us two cocktails, yellowish and greenish, in dainty glasses.

"Can I ask you a question?"

"Of course," she says.

"Is this a money-laundering operation or what?"

The waitress puts her hands up. It is impossible to get drunk.

"How do you clean your money?" the calf's brain guy says.

"How do you clean yours?" I say.

"I work at Goldman Sachs."

I laugh.

I never thought of there being anything out here before. I never thought of it at all. It was an outer ring. I catch sight of us in a warehouse window. We're wearing costumes.

"Someone's going to stab us," I say.

"Not anymore," the art guy says.

At a party there are people suspended from the rafters by hooks in their backs. Their flesh is stretched. I forgot this was even a holiday. The art guy brings a girl into the bathroom with us.

"This is Louisa. She's in some of my photos. The New York series."

She's wearing a sweatshirt that says I'M A FUCKING ZOMBIE.

"No," I say.

I can do bumps through the nose holes but I push up my mask so the art guy can see my face.

"No doubles," I say.

"Why not?" he says.

I go into my building and the light's out in the stairwell between three and four. There's a guy coming toward me and I think about mugging him.

"Hey," he says.

"Hey," I say.

I come out later and everything's blaring again.

I watch the ex-Ranger. I watch him walk into the cop bar and decide to sit down beside me.

"Listen, I can't pay your rent," the ex-Ranger says.

"Okay," I say.

"How many other guys pay your rent?"

"Four."

He laughs. I hold my face in my hand, looking at him.

"Right now," I say.

The bartender comes up and leans on his forearms in front of us. The ex-Ranger takes his phone out of his pocket. He puts it on the bar. I feel happy. Like this is what I wanted to happen. I light a cigarette and point it at him.

"Cherry Bomb for me and whatever this alcoholic wants."

The ex-Ranger lives in Queens, which is truly mystifying. He lives in one room above a store on an avenue. His apartment's almost as empty as mine. The closet is locked. When he kisses me everything sucks away, as if we are the only things in space. It makes half of me hate him.

Once in the snow, at two or three in the morning, I saw a toddler struggling to stay upright, trailing after his grandmother, who was half a block in front of him. This was in Chinatown in the 1990s.

I snort another VERSACE bag. I think how I will see snow again. If I had a baby I would kill it. I would kill it before it was born because it's the right thing to do.

At Agent Provocateur a salesgirl laces me into an elaborate corset.

"You can take off the hip panels if you want."

I look at myself in the mirror. I touch the two half-moons jutting from my waist. They make me seem more like a machine than a girl.

"No, I like them," I say.

While he's signing the receipt I stand beside the guy who buys me things but with a good whore's etiquette look the other way.

———

The junk-bond guy lives in a classic six. We're in the maid's room off the kitchen. He uses it as an office. He smokes in here and when my face is close to the couch it smells deliciously like cigarettes.

"You look like a mean doll," he says.

"Thank you," I say.

7

I can't stand having my feet touched. In the pedicure bath I cringe and flinch and what I want to do is kick the girl in the face. It makes me feel unguarded, like she could murder me. On my fingernails I get upside-down hearts, matte black like chalkboards. The points of my nails are their tails.

This wallpaper is marbled like meat. The bathroom we were in earlier was banana-patterned. It was scratch-n-sniff. I rub coke on my gums and teeth. I touch the wall and the club's bass goes through my palms and into my arms. I flip my hair. I look over my shoulder at the calf's brain guy. I have an obsession with symmetry. I think it is completely misleading. I smile at him.

Behind black theater curtains the gallery is all screens. On every screen there is a different person playing a different instrument in a different room of a decrepit mansion. I watch a woman playing a harp in a library.

"There are stars exploding around you and there's nothing, nothing you can do."

I look at him.

"That's what they're singing. I read it on the wall," the art guy says.

"Well, that's true."

In the middle of the gallery there are two screens where they are all on the porch of the house, singing together, but then they sound cacophonous. That's true, too. I think I'm the only person who has spent every second of my life with me. Inside of me the heroin turns a little and I think I might vomit.

"I'm hungry," I say.

I drop my bag on the ex-Ranger's floor and stumble over to the closet and try to open it.

"Why is this locked?" I say.

"What are you doing?" he says.

"I want to hang up my coat."

"Why?"

I tug on the door handle.

"What's in here?" I say.

"Stop."

"Bodies?"

He cages me. He backs me up against the closet and puts his hands on either side of my head.

"Guns?"

"No," he says.

I let my fake fur slide to my wrists.

"I know what it is," I say.

"What?"

I have my legs over my head. The wax lady blows on a wax-dipped Popsicle stick.

"Where do you find so many white outfits?" I say.

"Macy's," she says.

I ride the escalators of the Time Warner Center with the guy who buys me things. Because it is a shopping mall it reminds me of Dubai, but lacking the grandness of vision. The restaurant is behind a heavy door. There is a treetop panorama of Central Park. I think of it as unreal, as a projection for our visual entertainment. The waiter presses his palms together. He looks at me with complicity.

"Good afternoon. Sparkling today?"

"Yeah," the guy who buys me things says.

When my UAE residence visa expired I could have bought another one, like I had always done before, and a labor card, for a job in an office I never showed up for, but I didn't.

"I don't want water," I say.

At the exact speed the junk-bond guy licks a line up my pussy I arch my back and moan for him.

Around the earth are four dead rings of deserts, hot and cold, and the Arabian Desert is just one of them. It's a waterless ocean where storms of only wind blow the sand into waves. When I was in Dubai I expected to die out there one day, any day, of exposure and dehydration, as much as I expected to live.

I get my teeth bleached. I watch a tiny TV while a blue light shines into my peeled-open mouth. I think of the Sheikh and half of me hates him, too. The same half that hates the ex-Ranger.

"You can only eat white food for twenty-four hours," the dental assistant says.

"I'm just not going to eat at all," I say.

She unclips my blue bib.

"Good plan," she says.

I have always given myself a year to quit: heroin, whoring. Again and again on a different day I wake up in New York.

8

Mondays I have the calf's brain guy, Tuesdays the art guy, Thursdays the guy who buys me things, Fridays the junk-bond guy. I tell the ex-Ranger I can only see him on Wednesdays.

At the gym I take a dance class. At one point all the girls around me drop onto their hands and pop their pussies in the air. I stand there with my hands on my hips. I have stripped out of necessity, as a means to an end, and that's it. The TODAY girl is there. She's in the locker room.

"Hey," she says.

"Not today," I say.

"I want to punch you in the face."

In a nebulous way I wait for this. I cross my ankles behind the calf's brain guy's head.

"It's an extra grand."

"Fine," he says.

The best way to brace yourself is to think of something else.

———

I sit on the railing of the crooked balcony. He's in a puffy coat lounged in the lawn chair in the long-haired AstroTurf. We're both wearing sunglasses. Mine are so pink. He grins at me.

"I want to take pictures of you," the art guy says.

I grin back.

"No," I say.

"Yo."

The delivery guy tilts his head.

"Your eye," he says.

"I got in a fight."

He scrunches up his nose like something smells horrible, like serious dog shit.

"You're white."

I shut the door in his face.

Bruising is an unpredictable thing. The design is never the same. This time I have one Cleopatra eye. A purple Cleopatra that is shiny with Bacitracin.

At the cop bar the ex-Ranger dances for me. He feeds five dollars into the jukebox. I turn around on the stool and spread my legs. I lean back on my elbows and cock my head.

"I don't know what that is," I say.

The bartender throws a dollar at him. The ex-Ranger wipes his thumb across my cheekbone.

"Is that a shiner?"

I look at my concealer on him.

"Fucking MAC," I say.

"What?" he says.

"My makeup."

———

The ex-Ranger does not have a bed. I get up from his futon. His bathroom feels unheated. I avoid his mirror. When I come out his locked closet is open. He's standing beside it with a black pistol in his hand.

"You know how to shoot a gun?" he says.

"Yeah," I say.

He goes over to my bag and puts the Glock inside.

"What are you thinking about?"

"Your cock," I say.

The guy who buys me things smiles. I stand in front of the hotel room's full-length mirror wearing only the earrings he bought me. They're heavy. They brush my collarbone. I'm smiling at myself. Because he's right behind me.

I smoke in the maid's room with the junk-bond guy. I cross my legs on top of his.

"Why do we all go on living?" I say.

"I don't know. Inertia."

"Accretion."

I twist one of my big earrings. The junk-bond guy laughs.

"Like in a financial sense?" he says.

"No, because we're just adding days, not value. Every day we're alive makes it harder to die."

There's a pause. Unlike strippers, who should be happy, prostitutes should be sad but not too sad. It holds the attention longer. He pats my knee.

"I've got to kick you out soon. I'm sorry."

I was with a Siberian girl in a bathroom doing coke. We were doing one of those parties where the next day our thighs would burn too much to use stairs.

"Did you think you were going to be a nanny?" she said.

Her English was fucked-up but that's what she meant.

"No," I said.

The weekend is back to Saturday and Sunday. When I first arrived in Dubai it was Thursday and Friday, and then after five or so years it was changed by the government to Friday and Saturday, to be more Westernized. The weekend is for wives and real girlfriends. I clean my makeup brushes and hang them upside down on coat hangers with rubber bands because I care what happens to them.

9

In black-hole theory if someone fell into one, like an astronaut, he wouldn't feel a thing until he hit the bottom. That could take seconds or lifetimes. It is unlikely he would realize just before he was crushed to nothing that he was strung out like a string. I realize it, theoretically.

I'm in Duane Reade and I can't decide. I feel paralyzed. A woman walks up beside me. I want her to force my hand.
"Should I get the spicy tuna?" I say.
"I don't think you should eat that," she says.
I grab the salmon instead.

"You look good," the calf's brain guy says.
"Why wouldn't I?" I say.
Our waitress brings over a birdcage filled with fried chicken.

I'm shivering on the art guy's crooked balcony. It's morning. The skyline's missing. It's so foggy that across the river it's like Manhattan is gone, totally obliterated. Our building, when I was a kid, had a mezzanine floor that smelled like cabbage, like that was what every apartment's cooking boiled down to. A few weeks ago I asked the art guy what happened to Stuyvesant Town and he said "mezzanine debt." Maybe now it smells like something else.

I want to kill everyone in Whole Foods. This girl in front of me doesn't know how to walk. She's blocking the fresh ricotta. I ram my cart into her. She gasps. She turns over her shoulder, looking outraged.

"Yeah, move," I say.

My stove is a stranger. Finally I get down on my hands and knees and light the burner under the oven with my lighter.

I heft the tinfoil pan in my hands.

"I made you lasagna," I say.

"Why?" he says.

The ex-Ranger has a drawer full of plastic forks. While he eats he puts his hand on top of mine.

"This is good."

"Everything I put in my mouth tastes like a different kind of nothing," I say.

He laughs. I pull the Glock out of my bag and put it on his kitchen table.

"I don't need a gun."

"You might," he says.

I sit on the edge of a hotel bed with a large pink box on my knees. I look up at the guy who buys me things. I consider whether or not I would recognize him if we crossed on the street.

"Thank you," I say.

The junk-bond guy takes me for ice cream even though it's too cold. We sit on a bench along the wall. We're the only customers. He gives me his overcoat and it drapes over my shoulders. A few times I have practiced stabbing melons. All I have is surprise. If a man wants to pin me down by the neck he will. I lick his chocolate. He licks my vanilla.

I have not been this cold in fifteen years. I go to Macy's and buy a puffy coat that is only white. I was just fucking him, too, the Sheikh, no fee. He was my boyfriend. I hate that I'm thinking about the ex-Ranger when I'm alone.

The Sheikh wasn't really a sheikh. He did not wear a kandura but one of three white suits. He taught me how to belly dance. He opened his white jacket and rolled his white hips.

I put a ten on the counter and look at the bodega guy. He wiggles his fingers at me. I put down four more. He hands me the cigarettes.

10

I get Rorschach nails.
"What do you see?"
"I don't want to answer that question," I say.
The girl looks at the splotches she's made.
"Crows," she says.

The stamp's a one-way arrow. I make my face pissy.
"Editorializing is the worst," I say.
"Whatever," the delivery guy says.
He walks away before I can shut the door in his face.

"Just give me a couple adjectives."
"Fuck adjectives," I say.
The bartender is offended.
"Look, the way this place works is you describe what kind of drink you want and then I make you something."
He points to the chalkboard behind his head. There is a truly unhelpful list of words.
"Just give me a Sex on the Beach," I say.
"So, *vulgar* and *juvenile*," the bartender says.

I find them on the chalkboard: VULGAR and JUVENILE.

"Exactly."

"Two of those," the calf's brain guy says.

I look at him. When I was dumb I felt smug when a man started to become susceptible to me.

The art guy has his camera out. He keeps trying to point it at me.

"I'm going to throw it over the balcony."

"I'm going to throw you over the balcony," he says.

We're in his glass apartment. I'm on his hard black couch.

"You're addicted to male attention," he says.

He takes off the lens cap.

"Would you say that's why you're a prostitute?"

"I don't think that's it," I say.

I stand up and move out of view.

The ex-Ranger pulls his fingers through my hair.

"I want to take you out to dinner," he says.

I open my eyes and look at the skin of his chest.

"Okay," I say.

The cardboard tube in this roll of toilet paper doesn't go all the way through. It's cut in half. The rest of the roll is a mass of wadded white. It's abnormal like a book where one of the pages is overgrown, where the machine missed it. It's freakish. It's always supposed to be the same. I have to throw it away because I can't stop looking at it.

On the train I stare at the guy across from me. I start counting. He looks at me, twice, and then he sort of smiles. Seven seconds. I close my eyes.

————

I order a stuffed cabbage from the Polish diner. I make them deliver. I eat on the couch and listen to the building. The guy below's chasing a girl around his apartment. I hear them running back and forth. Her light footsteps followed by his heavy ones. She yells help but not like she means it. Otherwise it is quiet.

I don't see the guy who buys me things or the junk-bond guy. Instead we text feverishly. It's Thanksgiving. For four days I don't go outside. Heroin is a justifying drug. Whatever I decide to do or don't do it agrees with me calmly.

"I have to go home for Eid."

"Why?" I said.

"I have to slaughter a cow. I promised my mother," the Sheikh said.

He waved his hand in the air and left it there. We were high, in the rush.

"Okay," I said.

//

In an Argentine movie a man gives something to a girl.

"I'm going to give you something."

She is maybe his daughter.

"Here," he says.

For a long time I don't know what it is. I like this.

"Why can't she take my order?" I say.

"Why can't I take your order?"

In the Polish diner I position myself in my chair so that I am not looking at the waitress but the blue woman behind the register.

"Mom," the waitress says.

"Mom?" I say.

I take a yoga class at the gym and at the end we do not lie on the floor for five minutes like we're corpses. The teacher prays her hands. She bows over her lap.

"Namaste," the teacher says.

I am irate. The TODAY girl is not in the locker room so I can't ignore her.

The dining room is the drawing room of what used to be a private mansion. The tables are huge and white-clothed and few and floating. There is a hush.

"I want to punch you in the face again," the calf's brain guy says.

I look across a swath of carpet at the couple closest to us and then I make a face. I don't need an extra grand. I have enough money.

The art guy is out of town. I walk through Union Square. I stop in front of a street kid. His cardboard says WILL FUCK HOT GIRLS FOR GOOD DRUGS.

"Are you in an awesome band?"

"What?" he says.

I kick his sign with one of my teacup heels.

"That's how that works."

He looks up at me and smirks.

"Yeah, I'm the lead singer of Maybe You Can Suck My Dick but I Haven't Decided Yet."

"You look more like the drummer."

"Fuck you," he says.

"You want to get a drink?" I say.

"As I'm sure you know, the universe is expanding, spreading thinner and thinner. Eventually it will spread too thin for physics. That's when everything will pixelate."

He's doing tequila shots. After each one he does a little dance.

"Yeah, I know," he says.

"Then it will snap. The universe."

"Can I ask you a question?" the street kid says.

"Of course," I say.

"You're a pro, right?"

I cross my legs. I feign disdain.

"What?"

"Do you know who's going to rape you and steal your shit? Like, do you get a feeling in your gut?"

I flick my Cherry Bomb cup at the trash. He does half his dance and then stops.

"No, you can never tell," I say.

A woman in an abaya, a niqab, and gloves, all black, came up to me.

"I'm sorry," I said.

I pointed at the previously spotless sidewalk that was now spotted everywhere with my blood.

The bodega guy is staring at my black eye.

"Remember when you guys sold coke in here?" I say.

"Fourteen dollars," he says.

"Maybe I should go on jobs with you."

I look at the ex-Ranger's suit.

"Like security?"

He shrugs. He drinks his beer.

"It's not safe, carrying around cash like that," the ex-Ranger says.

In Dubai I had a driver who was sometimes the Sheikh. I wouldn't make him wait outside while I got fucked. I would call him when I was done. But still he took too long to pick me up.

"I thought you were going to take me out to dinner," I say.

At three a.m. we eat ninety-nine-cent pizza standing on the street.

"This doesn't count," the ex-Ranger says.

When he moves his head a neon blur follows him.

"Tomorrow night."

"I'm busy," I say.

I leave the guy who buys me things at the fake orgy. A crowd of white-masked people runs past chasing a pregnant woman. I go the other way. Earlier there was a bar with shots sitting on it and I try to find it. Again someone grabs me. A woman in a long gown drags me into a small room. She whispers something portentous in my ear, pressing her tits into me. She's an actress. I look at the real bed we're sitting on.

"Can I lie down?" I say.

We're at this immersive play and there are no seats.

Probably the junk-bond guy has lived in this apartment since before I was born. We are making out in the maid's room and the floorboards are creaking and I have the awful urge to tell him this, that I was born just down the FDR at Beth Israel in the dark in the summertime.

"Where'd they take him?"

"Beth Israel."

"Yeah, man, Beth Israel's where everybody goes to die."

My battery is dead and I have to walk down the block without headphones. I look at the two winos as I pass by.

"Mami," one says.

"God bless you," the other one says.

I'm walking by Stuy Town when I see a woman who I swear is my mother. I turn around on First Avenue. I cut off a guy hailing a taxi.

"Cunt," he says.

"Where are you going?" the driver says.

"What?" I say.

12

"What?" I say.

The calf's brain guy stops looking at me sincerely. He resumes texting.

"What," he says.

When the waiter comes the calf's brain guy orders a hamburger, medium, with cheese, even though there is squab on the menu.

"What's wrong with you?" I say.

The art guy is wearing a Buddhist monk's saffron robes. He's fucking two Thai prostitutes in a hotel room with white tile floor so everything can be bleached. His head is shaved. It still is. I tap the space bar with the tip of my nail.

"Don't worry, I got what I paid for."

I look at him.

"Even two of them weren't as good as you," he says.

"Do you tell the hedge fund that you're going to Bangkok to fuck bar girls and film it?"

I run my nail down the opening in his shirt.

"I'm not really as professional as you think I am. Remember when you said that? And that's in Chiang Mai."

I button one of the art guy's buttons.

"Show me your Z-Pak," I say.

I was terrified of the first man who paid me. I was eighteen. It was my first time overseas. He took me to a restaurant that I would learn to make fun of but only later. I was convinced they could tell, the driver, the waiters, the hotel staff, him. I wanted to appear professional. I was not terrified of the man who tried to kill me. I was thirty-two. For too many years I had escaped the bad luck of whores.

"In Dubai only men wear all white. Women wear black."
The wax lady pats my thigh with her white-gloved hand.
"Legs over your head," she says.

I assume before I knew him the ex-Ranger was all muscle. His full weight is on top of me. I can breathe but I feel like I can't. He could hurt me but he won't. I wake up with him again.

I'm on the Barneys elevator with puffy-lipped women. They look at me dismissively. They are highly contoured in an out-of-it way. But one time someone must have told them: marry a dentist in Jersey and just be happy. I imagine my mother saying that—dentist, New Jersey—and then I laugh. They think I'm laughing at them. The guy who buys me things is behind me. His hands are on my waist.
"Excuse us," he says.
We get off on the expensive floor.

The junk-bond guy and I both sleep through the movie. When we come out it is snowing. He is walking and I'm standing there. He looks over his shoulder.
"Kasia," he says.

I take a new series of photos of my ass. At best I have ten years left. A middle-aged woman is a mother. A middle-aged whore is walking the streets or dead.

"Ooh, HERMÈS."

I grin at the delivery guy. He nods at my eye.

"My mom used to hide us in the bathroom and when my stepfather tried to take the screws out the knob she'd stab a knife in the doorjamb."

I nod at him.

"That's smart," I say.

13

This girl is known for copying artists. The appointment before me gets cows and hibiscus flowers. When it's my turn I put my hands on the table.

"I want fifty randomly placed points connected by straight lines," I say.

The nail girl looks this up on her phone.

"Insanity," she says.

"No, it's not. It's logic."

He grabs me by the ankle.

"How much for a month?" he says.

I shrug at the calf's brain guy.

"I don't do that," I say.

I'm sucking off the art guy and he's being an asshole and not coming so I sit back on my heels for a second and look at Manhattan. Cities are inert and don't have feelings. I am the one with feelings.

The ex-Ranger's ceiling is pressed tin and though it's muffled by decades of paint the pattern is still there. It was rare to be anywhere in

Dubai without a pattern. There were dense Islamic patterns everywhere. Mosques are empty patterned buildings. The Muslim girls could charge the most and they had henna tattoos that crawled up their arms like delicate, intricate snakes.

At a dermatologist I get a B_{12} shot in my ass. I try to feel fucking great.

I almost buy myself this leather jacket. It has long fringe down the back.

"It'll last you forever," the salesgirl says.

I put it back.

The Dior store has a room with a fireplace. Tendrils climb the walls to the ceiling in 3-D. The guy who buys me things sits on a couch. I stand in front of him with my legs parted.

"I want you to fuck me on this carpet," I say.

"We'll take the furry one downstairs," the guy who buys me things says.

The salesguy is discreet in a corner.

"Right away," the salesguy says.

The guy who buys me things buys a purse I dislike that I will try to remember to carry most but not every time I see him. A good whore is an empty pattern like me.

I have not been in the living room before. In his living room the junk-bond guy has a baby coffin. It is in the shape of a Nike sneaker and it is painted red.

"Amy got it in Ghana."

His wife is a collector of weird art. I think I know many things about many wives.

"It's a coffin," the junk-bond guy says.

The lid is open.

"I know," I say.

I get fucked on the floor and not the couch. I assume the logic is that he sits on this couch with his wife. Logic is always evolving.

After the Sheikh disappeared I let a Qatari man buy me for one year. He rented an apartment that I never left. When he wasn't there I would lie on the bed, in the air-conditioning, with the curtains open, and think of the sun out there, just burning somewhere. One time I thought this was true happiness, and maybe it was.

I watch a circle circle.

14

The ginger that came with this Duane Reade sushi is kind of fucked-up, withered. I eat it anyway.

There's a line for the showers. The TODAY girl is just ahead of me. She turns around though she has no reason to.
   "Are you following me?" she says.
   "Please," I say.
   She's following me. In the shower I find the mole on my rib cage that I am sometimes sure is cancerous and I almost black out.

I get my hair cut. In the mirror I watch my face shift infinitesimally. Eventually I shouldn't be able to recognize myself. I should become one of those words that are suddenly foreign. The Arabic of the Gulf was like music because I never understood. I moved through sound.
   "Can I take a photo for my Instagram?" the hairdresser says.
   She's done. I still see myself.
   "No, thank you," I say.

———

The calf's brain guy is back to being cold to me. We're in a restaurant with a perfect view of Jersey.

"I'll have a Fernet-Branca. She'll probably have a milkshake."

The waiter looks at me. His face looks like it could go either way.

"Milkshake," I say.

The dessert comes with a gold-leaf dove perched on its crust. I put the whole bird in my mouth for him.

"Did you go to work today? Did you make a lot of money?"

"Yeah," he says.

There is the softest smell of shit as I lick the art guy's asshole.

"How do you do it?" the ex-Ranger says.

"Do what?"

"Fuck for money."

We're lying flat on our backs on his futon. I have a standard thing I say. In Dubai there was an ex-Ranger, but not a Sheikh, regularly.

"Heroin. Coke is for stripping," I say.

Earth's largest flower is a parasite that blooms fifteen pounds of petals that look like rotting flesh. When it is most alive it smells dead. I think I'm the other way. If the stain on my ceiling is a person it is definitely a man. He is wearing a suit and carrying a briefcase. He thinks what we have is a symbiotic relationship.

I try to go to the Polish diner. Then I try to go to Duane Reade. I go into the bodega and look at the guy.

"Why is everything closed?" I say.

"Christmas," he says.

———

I eat a bag of Bugles. I snort a bag of HERMÈS. They text me.
"Where is my Christmas present, what the fuck?" I text to all of them.
Then I don't reply again.

We were on the beach. It was Eid, the first one we spent together. There were fireworks. There were irritating kids everywhere.
"My sons will never be that misbehaved," the Sheikh said.
"Your sons?" I said.
I laughed.
"Yeah, when I get married I'm going to have twenty sons."
He grinned at me. My face must have betrayed me. It was dark so he kissed me.
"Baby, you and me are just fantasy," he said.

15

It is open again, the Polish diner. I order a stuffed cabbage to go. I smile at the blue woman and show my teeth.

"Happy holidays," I say.

She just nods at me.

"Eight dollars," she says.

I text them all to find out when they will be back in the city.

"Next week," they all text, except ER.

The ex-Ranger's at the cop bar. He flips the hair off my shoulder.

"Do you hate these forced holidays?" I say.

He beams at me.

"Where are the drugs?" he says.

We live in his bed that is not even a bed, combining and recombining into different shapes but staying one thing. I scratch the ex-Ranger's back. The rhythm saves me from being sick.

"People think what I do is easy. Actually it's exhausting," I say.

"I don't think people think it's easy. I think they think it's lazy."
I keep doing too much so we can both be high.

We rub our itching noses.
"Stop," I say.
"Stop," he says.

He kisses my pussy forever but I can't feel a thing. All my nerves are dull. I make my inner thighs shudder. I fake it to make him feel good, not to ensure I get my full rate. I say his name.

"Unaffected," he says.
"What?"
"Everyone else is walking around like they're unaffected."
His radiators rattle and his voice is hoarse like mine.
"Not you," the ex-Ranger says.
I imagine me in a mall in Dubai and him in the mountains of Afghanistan, concurrently.
"Uninfected," I say.
"Okay."
I imagine us every day moving in different, useless formations.
"They're walking around like they're uninfected. Everyone else."

He squeezes our clammy bodies together.
"You make me feel lucky," he says.
I feel a rush of guilt that is another kind of nauseous. I should go, I think. I mean it but I don't leave.

The ex-Ranger is a security guard at the Bank of America Tower, a skyscraper that didn't use to exist. He spends his day staring through a glass wall at the street.

"You are fucking me on NYE," is a text on my phone from CBG.

"I have to go home," I say.

As soon as I stand up I have to run to the bathroom. I puke twice in the ex-Ranger's toilet and my throat burns.

Like New York, winter, when you are away from it for so long, can become an abstract thing, a thing that could solve problems. My skin is so dry it's peeling off. I cover my whole face in Aquaphor. I slather my thigh in vitamin E. Not even the ex-Ranger has asked about the scars. I don't own a spoon. I stick my stuffed-cabbage fork in my yogurt.

Maybe he thought he knew what he was doing. But the man who tried to kill me missed my femoral artery.

"You should go home. What is wrong with America?" the nurse said.

It's late. Duane Reade is closed. Walgreens is open. They have a self-service frozen-yogurt station. They have a selection of toppings. The chocolate pretzels are jammed. I find the security guard and look at him helplessly. Before I leave I steal a lot of spoons.

I hear the other girls screaming. There is screaming everywhere. It must be midnight. I put my foot up on the wall of the bathroom stall and stare at my sparkly tights and drink my champagne for a while.

"I had to kiss somebody else," the calf's brain guy says.

"Please think of how I can make it up to you," I say.

16

The calf's brain guy and I both have small spotted quail's eggs. They are already cracked in half. We pour them into our ramen.

"I'm going to drop my napkin," he says.

When he looks under the table I open my legs. I have chopsticks in one hand, swirling runny goo into my broth. With the other I play with my clit. He sits back up. I lick my fingers.

"I'm going to piss on you later."

"Okay," I say.

We sit on the benches across from MoMA smoking cigarettes and watching clenched people pass.

"I remember when most women in New York had frizzy hair."

"I grew up in Greenwich. Everybody has the same hair always," the art guy says.

I turn my freezing face to his. I kick him with my bootie.

"That was touching," I say.

"Who were you with on New Year's?"

"What day of the week was that?" I say.

The ex-Ranger's chewing a toothpick. He looks at the bartender and points the toothpick at me.

"Cherry Bomb for her. She's exhausted," he says.

I draw my finger down the center of the ex-Ranger's face.

"I'm not lazy," I say.

"I am," he says.

As soon as I walk into the gym I see the TODAY girl. She is using a machine that is rowing in place.

"Hey," she says.

I have my headphones in and I walk past her like I didn't hear. In the yoga class we are supposed to be thinking nothing. I'm thinking I can feel the liveness of everyone in this room, flat on our backs, in tight new-year rows, and it is a very strong vibration.

After I made a man come many times in one night I got what I thought was a great compliment.

"You are life," he said.

It made me feel purposeful.

I crawl across the hotel bed. The guy who buys me things is sitting up with his legs wide. I stand up on my knees and put my hands on my hips.

"What?" he says.

"You haven't bought me anything today."

He slaps me hard across the face.

The junk-bond guy picks up my furry purse from the living room floor. He weighs it in his hand.

"What's in here?" he says.

"A gun. This is a dangerous business," I say.

My Christmas gifts are mostly cash. I like the ex-Ranger more because he got me nothing. I text DG.

"15 MIN," DG texts.

I watch a Portuguese movie that's as at rest as a painting. I text DG.

"15 MIN," DG texts.

"Who comes up with the stamps?" I say.

"Me," the delivery guy says.

I shut the door in his face. It's a picture of a passenger plane plus DRONE.

17

A pattern is not like an echo. Each subsequent repetition is not less than what came before it.

The hot tub in the floor is full of naked girls. They look stocked, though it is meant to be spontaneous. The water looks green. Like it's infected, I think, and they're pretending not to notice. I'm standing at the edge with the calf's brain guy. I can't hear anything. He says something.

"You're right," I say.

He moves his drink to his other hand and threads his fingers through mine.

"Look, my new coke guy has business cards."

He shows me. It says RON'S LIMOUSINE CAR SERVICE 9 P.M. TO 5 A.M.

"That's funny," I say.

The art guy has already told me he's been up for three days. I think about how he's never going to come.

"Take off everything," the art guy says.

I grab the hem of my dress and peel it over my head.

"I'm going to come," the art guy says.

I roll my eyes at the city. My hands are pressed against his glass wall and more than I see the Con Ed stacks I see my face, superimposed.

At one point I get a lot of satisfaction from tweezing my eyebrows and at another point it's from flossing my teeth. Fucking cocaine, I think.

We were in the bathroom and then we were in the bedroom. We were in the kitchen and then we were in the living room. I'm on my hands and knees on his shiny floor. I need to smoke. I need to pee.

"I'm going to come," the art guy says.

I come out of the bathroom and the zombie girl is standing in the art guy's kitchen.

"You remember Louisa?"

"No," I say.

The zombie girl crouches at my feet and licks my pussy. I squeeze my tits and stare in the eyes of the art guy. He's on his black couch, frantically jerking off. I refuse to come.

I'm out on the balcony with the zombie girl. She pops a cube of bubblegum in her mouth, though she's still smoking a cigarette.

"Shit," she says.

Inside, the art guy finally gets his projector working. Speeding cars flash onto the white wall. It's specially painted to sharpen the picture. He went on and on about it one time. In the glass room he shoots his arms up. He's naked. The zombie girl turns her head back to me.

"Barnard is really expensive."

"I don't care," I say.

It was purely for financial reasons that he funded the insurgency. It was an investment in future governments where he could control the purse strings. It was about doubling his money like anything else. The Sunni thing was just a cover, or a tool, or a manipulation. He went on and on about it, this coked-up Saudi. I don't think the other girl was listening. I was listening. Doubles were competitive and I had to be the best.

The zombie girl is gone and I'm still here. I look at the art guy's dick. I hate it. I put it in my mouth.

I text GBT and JBG to cancel. I text ER: "I know I wasn't at the bar. I was at work."

The art guy shows up in the mirror behind me. He bends me over at the waist and sticks his dick in me. He comes almost immediately and kind of softly. He drops his head on my back, breathing hard. I put my hands down on the lid of the toilet and let him lie there for a while.

Coke is feeling everything. Even feeling one thing is unbearable. On my couch I look at the twin airplanes on my kneecaps, where the two DRONE bags are flat. For a while the earth might drift after the black dwarf that used to be the sun. I see the Sheikh point his finger and follow its trail.

18

It is snowing again. I wander Midtown at night in the muteness.

I steel myself while the nail girl massages my feet. When we get to hands I ask her what to do. She says letters, like knuckle tattoos.
"Two four-letter words or one eight-letter word. That's best."
"Okay, *wall* and *door*," I say.
After a second the nail girl laughs like she is truly happy.

At the Polish diner the blue woman is taking orders. The new waitress is nowhere. I decide to stay. I sit at a table and wait for her. For a while she ignores me.
"Yes."
"Why don't you remember me?" I say.
Her eyes are squinty like mine and when she narrows them they seem to go away. Briefly it's like a bluebird died on her face. She flicks her hand at me.
"I see a lot of people," she says.
I flick my hand at her.
"Bigos," I say.

When I was a little girl my mother dressed me up in outlandish outfits and walked me down the street. Sometimes older girls laughed at me.

"They're jealous of your confidence," my mother said.

They're jealous of my confidence, I thought. Confused because it was not mine, it was hers.

On the train platform all the women look at me hurtfully and I know I look good today.

For the sake of the calf's brain guy I'm pretending like I've never been to this play. I go off alone again. The top floor is the infirmary. There are rows of hospital beds. I take off my mask and lie down. It's cool and there is the ambient sound of distant wailing. I wake up surrounded. People with the same white face are staring down at me. They are waiting silently like I'm one of the actors and they are expecting me to lead them somewhere. They want me to advance the story. If I just sat up they would follow.

"Guys, I'm going to lie here for a little while longer," I say.

The art guy is at that coke point where he's talking about his father, who is his boss, the manager of the hedge fund.

"He thinks I'm a drug addict."

We both sniff up our drip reflexively.

"You should fuck me on his desk," I say.

The art guy laughs wildly. I laugh, too. I feel jittery. I want to change locations. I jump off his crooked balcony onto AstroTurf.

"Let's go now."

"Not now," he says.

The ex-Ranger runs his thumbs over my fingernails.

"WALL and DOOR?"

"It's an inside joke," I say.

"What's the joke?"

I jerk my hands away.

"You don't get to know that," I say.

I come out of the bathroom and the guy who buys me things is getting dressed. A pale blue Tiffany box is on the hotel bed. I suddenly remember I didn't see him last week, that he must think I'm pissed about some unknown thing. I think I could ask him for something else. He looks sideways from knotting his tie.

"Today was Bonus Day," he says.

I sit on the edge of the baby coffin to pull on my thigh-highs. I've already told the art guy where I grew up so I answer the junk-bond guy's question.

"Sacred Heart, on scholarship."

"I went to Collegiate, full tuition," the junk-bond guy says.

"I get to ask you something. Not now but later," I say.

"Deal."

I dig my nails into my legs until my eyes open.

19

In the bathroom of this restaurant I suck the dick of the calf's brain guy. I wet my finger and swirl it indolently around his asshole. I don't ask what his bonus was even though I want to know.

I look at a life-size woman sewn from inside-out coyote skin. I look at the white card: COYOTE'S SUIT TO DISGUISE HIMSELF AS ME. The next booth is only tinfoil animals.

"They're solid all the way through. The artist just keeps wrapping and wrapping. He starts out with a whole room full of tinfoil, like a whole warehouse, and he ends up with just this."

A gallery guy is talking to the art guy.

"How much do they go for?" the art guy says.

I wander over to a wall of pinned-up baby dolls. They have knitted face masks and doors cut into their stomachs with other, tinier babies hidden inside. I feel surrounded by sickness. The art guy comes up behind me. He puts his two palms on my ass.

"This is shit you shouldn't fuck with, like those African fetish things you have to menstruate on every month or they'll kill you," I say.

The art guy points across the art fair.

"Those are over there."

I wake up scared. I touch the futon beside me and there's no one there. I find the ex-Ranger in his bathroom. He has shaving cream all over his face.

"What are you doing?" I say.

I squint at him. I took out my contacts because I felt safe and now I can't see.

"Shaving," he says.

In the sink are all the black cuttings of his beard. I'm worried about the shape of his chin. I'm worried he will no longer remind me of the Sheikh.

"Why?"

"I can't sleep," he says.

I met the Sheikh through the coked-up Saudi. He was at one of the parties. There was something cheap about him that I liked immediately.

"You don't look like you belong here."

He was at the sushi buffet only eating the cucumber rolls.

"You do," he said.

An ancient woman bumps into me. She's wearing the same color lipstick as me, which is neon pink.

"Excuse you," she says.

"Cunt," I say.

We both look startled.

At his office the guy who buys me things has a private bathroom. He fucks me in front of his full-length mirror and it makes me technical. I calculate the tilt of my butt and tits. I adjust the angle of my head until my hair falls on my lower back and I am perfectly scooped out. The whole time I grin at him. Afterward I sit at his desk and look at the East River.

"So what do you think?" he says.

I shrug.

"It's not Goldman Sachs but there's nothing wrong with this place."

For the first time we're lying on the living room couch. It's chintzy and scentless and I'm looking at a two-man saw hanging on the wall above the mantel. It's not exactly the same shade of red as the baby coffin.

"Do you ever have to go into the office? Like when you start to wonder if this art is going to attack you?" I say.

"Only for board meetings," the junk-bond guy says.

"Is it in Midtown? Do you have a view of the river?"

"It is and we do."

I wake up and it's light outside. I wake up and it's dark outside. Across two razed lots in the midst of construction I can see the 405 East Fourteenth building of Stuy Town, from street to roof, where I used to live. I don't want to go outside where everything is moving too fast. The snow is the color of cigarette ash and I can't wear any of my suede shoes.

20

The calf's brain guy is eating calf's brain again. It makes me feel tender toward him.

"Okay, one month," I say.

The calf's brain guy flips a shishito pepper on the electric grill before he looks at me.

"I'm going to take your phone away."

I'm trying the Achilles tendon. I chew for a while and then I nod at him.

"15 MIN," DG texts.

I don't text anyone else. I think it is better to disappear and come back and see who stays.

I request the Pierre because its gaudiness reminds me of the Middle East. I shut the gold curtains and sit on the white bed.

The calf's brain guy tosses me a Wolford bag.

"Put them on," he says.

The tights are black satin, back-seamed. I bend over in front of him and run my hands up the backs of my legs. I laugh.

"I feel so slippery," I say.

I get down on my knees, disoriented and groggy. I open my mouth for his cock. He stops me. He pulls my head up by the hair.

"What are you not wearing?"

I look at myself between the robe. I'm not wearing anything.

"Tights," the calf's brain guy says.

"Tights," I say.

I go find the tights.

He comes in the morning before work. He comes in the evening after work. The time all around is mine. I decide I will get up and go to the bathroom in fifteen minutes. I look at the clock on the nightstand and it is two hours later.

The calf's brain guy's suit has thin stripes. I run the toe of my tights up one line until I get to his butt. I think about the Qatari man who bought me for a year. I was grateful to him. He made it possible for me to wallow in my grief. The calf's brain guy looks over his shoulder and smiles at me.

I shake my ass for him and drink out of the prosecco bottle. Sometimes he stops me to fuck me but then he sinks back into the armchair and jerks off again. I catch myself in the mirror, jiggling, two beats slower than the music, four beats, and I know me. I have yet to change.

The calf's brain guy pushes the room service cart in front of me. He sits down in the armchair.

"You want to watch me eat?"

"Yes," he says.

I'm not hungry at all. I butter a piece of toast. He crosses his legs and sips from his coffee cup.

"What are you going to do to me later?"

"None of your business," he says.

I think of the next thing I should say.

"How's work? Are you merging or acquiring anything this week?"

"Terrible. Yes."

"What did you get on Bonus Day?" I say.

"None of your business either."

I nick myself shaving and watch blood pour out of my ankle. I drop my foot in the bathwater so it will stop. When I get out I tape a cotton ball to my leg because I can't find a Band-Aid. I do it instinctively. The body and brain are every second conniving to stay alive.

I hear the key card in the slot and scramble. I press my face to the carpet. I hear the calf's brain guy come up to me. He kicks off his shoe. In the crack of my ass his sock foot is icy.

"Good," he says.

While he's fucking me I look in his eyes. It is impossible to remember the first lie I ever told. I don't know what it was but I know my mother believed it.

"Thank you," I say.

"For what?"

"Now all I have to do all day is think about you."

He smirks.

"You're welcome," the calf's brain guy says.

In this dream the ex-Ranger is wearing the Sheikh's white suit and he is standing in the middle of many different clubs, spliced together, in

Dubai. Logically, the Sheikh was a twitchy wire and the ex-Ranger should be splitting his suit in two, but he's not. I am myself.

"What do you do?" I say.

I open my eyes. The calf's brain guy is standing over me.

"Play with yourself," he says.

I touch him to make sure he's really there.

I loll around on the bed and slide my slick satin legs one over the other. He never came back after he slaughtered his cow. I told myself I wasn't waiting, that year with the Qatari man, but I was. I was waiting even after the man who tried to kill me. I roll myself in the covers and fantasize they are the arms of the ex-Ranger.

I sprawl on the floor of the shower while the calf's brain guy pees on me. His piss is hot and acid like any person's.

We share a hamburger. I sit on the edge of the bed and he sits in the armchair and we pass it back and forth over the hexagons of the carpet.

"Why is that a thing with rich men?"

"What?"

"Pissing on girls," I say.

The calf's brain guy shrugs.

"Money gives you choices," he says.

The calf's brain guy was just here and now he's here again. I stare at him. His face is in my face. I put my mouth on it.

"Who's the richest man you've ever fucked?" he says.

I giggle at this game.

From the TV I order Hollywood movies. Something is always going to happen next until it's not, which is the end. I keep hitting the button to see how much time is left. I have to finish a movie, even if I don't like it, or I can't stand myself. I lick ketchup off my tights.

"I called him the Sheikh."

"Who?" the calf's brain guy says.

"The richest man I ever fucked. Remember when you asked me that this morning?"

I feel his face tense up. It's in my tits.

"He was like a prince or something?"

"He pissed on me all the time," I say.

His hand on my skull gets tight. I close my eyes. It's true that there is a moment of suspense.

"I think about you," the calf's brain guy says.

His fist hits my face.

In the morning he doesn't show. The sun is insipid. I eat a French fry and look at it through the sheer curtain. Winter was wearing me down and I don't miss it. I do miss that futon with its thin mattress through which I could feel all the slats.

The nail girl has only the most basic shades.

"Pick a color," she says.

"Clambake," I say.

I sit on the edge of the bed in the bathrobe and she sits on the other side of a folding table attached to a folding chair that she brought with her. She does not look at my black eye. But when she touches my hands I feel her compassion. I don't say, "You know what it's like," and she also says nothing.

"Go in my purse and take whatever you want."

"What?" she says.

"For a tip."

I shake my nails at her.

"You didn't have gel. They're still wet," I say.

I ice my black eye with room-service ice: twenty minutes on, twenty minutes off. The nail girl only took five dollars, which was smart. Rich women do not hesitate to complain. I'm in this room so that's what I am. Tonight it's just me, no calf's brain guy.

"What do you do?" I said.

Because I was not in New York I could not ask right away. This was not even at the Saudi's party. We were drinking long black coffees at one of Dubai's Australian cafés.

"I make bombs," the Sheikh said.

I laughed.

"For the Saudi?"

He never pissed on me, the Sheikh. He had no money.

21

The calf's brain guy puts his hands on his hips.

"You need to let the maid in here."

"Why?" I say.

He puts his coat on again.

"Let's go downstairs to eat. Whatever that restaurant is. Where's your dress?"

I don't like this.

"I can't leave the room. I have rules."

He claps his hands.

"Get up," he says.

On the way back up, the elevator attendant refers to me as the calf's brain guy's wife and I look at the back of his face like it might crack. It is just us. I laugh. He doesn't react. He's wearing gloves and when the doors open he turns over his white hand.

"Thank you," I say.

I think I need my pussy waxed. I think that would make the calf's brain guy happy.

The calf's brain guy is rough with me. He drags me under the armpit. He holds me down by the neck and fucks me in the ass without any lube. The bathroom floor is wet.

"Tell me to come," he says.

He's angry.

We split a turkey club.

"Did you hack my phone?" I say.

"Why would I do that?" he says.

We look at each other poker-faced. He lets me eat all the potato chips.

He told me it was good.

"I'm a professional," I said.

His apartment was shitty. The singing of the muezzin was loud, close, dispelling the illusion I sometimes got that I wasn't really in a Muslim country. I looked at him like he might get up but he stayed between my legs.

"I'm an infidel," the Sheikh said.

I haven't seen the calf's brain guy since last night. I soak my tights in the sink. I wheel out the old food cart. I make the bed. From room service I order ice cream and a bikini wax.

"I'll connect you to a spa we recommend," the man says.

"I'm not leaving this room," I say.

I hear his key. I get just clear of where the door would hit me and sit on my ankles and put my hands on my knees like a pinup. The calf's brain guy just stops himself from tripping over me.

"Please fuck me," I say.

"Why else would I be here?" he says.

———

The ceiling of the Pierre is the smoothest paint job in the world. There is nothing on it embossed or painted or stained to interpret. I feel grateful. I run my fingers through his hair and graze his neck.

"You make me feel crazy," the calf's brain guy says.

I open the gold curtains but not the sheer and stand back from the window at a distance. A month is a twelfth of a year and a year is a hundredth or a sixtieth or a thirty-third of a life. I'm giving myself a sliver of time to wait for true happiness to come again. It's only a temporary evasion.

I ask the wax lady if she's from Brazil and she says yes. She's also wearing all white.

"Everything?"

"Everything."

"What happened to your eye?" she says.

The rush of serendipity goes away. I don't let her take whatever tip she wants.

I do a gradient cranberry smoky eye that is a sexy version of my bruising. I backcomb my hair. When I open the bathroom door I linger in the frame. The calf's brain guy is sitting on the edge of the bed eating my melted ice cream.

"Look at you," he says.

"Hey," I say.

He fucks me in a basic way and after he comes inside of me he rests his head in the space under my chin. I think he's making this complicated.

He leaves but right away he comes back in. I yank the tights back up.

"What if I wanted you for a year?" he says.

"I don't do that," I say.

He goes out again.

He comes back in the morning like he never broke his pattern. Like I'm not being punished anymore.

"You're in a good mood," he says.

"I'm always in a good mood."

The calf's brain guy makes a face.

"What?" I say.

We're both in the armchair. I'm giving him a lap dance. I stretch my leg so it's above our heads.

"Feelings are a weird thing," I say.

I have the front desk connect me with the Polish diner but they refuse to deliver uptown. I get irate with the blue woman. I would know her voice anywhere. She hangs up on me. I get connected to the closest Duane Reade. It's obvious that the girl who picks up the phone thinks I'm insane.

"Do you have spicy tuna or not?"

"We don't deliver," she says.

"A bellboy's going to pick it up," I say.

A broken pattern is no longer a pattern unless it is broken and picked up again in a consistent way. I hang up the phone.

The calf's brain guy ties me up in a loose way. It's easy to twist around and watch. I could get free if I wanted.

I tug on his ear.

"What?" he says.

"I think you're falling in love with me."

"Don't flatter yourself."

I notice his arm around me. The comforter is kicked down to our feet. It feels static like it's the middle of the night.

"Is your wife out of town?" I say.

"No," he says.

Earlier he said, "I make the rules." I laugh in my head.

I can't find my bathrobe so I drag the comforter off the bed and wrap it around me to answer the door. The bellboy holds out two plastic bags.

"Cherry vodka and Red Bull," he says.

"Yeah, thanks," I say.

I'm in the bath. The calf's brain guy is sitting on its edge. A glass tumbler is floating over my stomach. I taste like the ex-Ranger and me.

"I'm not falling in love with you," he says.

"Terrific," I say.

I was wrong. He's not like the Qatari man. He's like the men who blame me for their own emotions, which is not the worst kind.

He punches me in the kidneys and I throw up on him and he leaves.

I snort a bag of SPLENDA that is heroin, not fake sugar. I think fondly of the delivery guy. My brain blooms into the interior shapes of the Pierre, the circles and squares and hexagons. They feed on each other. They spread around corners faster than I can. I watch them unfold like a movie that will continue to play after I'm dead but not perpetually. Here is the burning sun and I don't feel comforted.

Maybe I have changed. Maybe it's me who's fucking this up. Maybe it's me who's making this dissimilar to how it was with the man from Qatar. I look at the clock on the nightstand. In four hours I have not changed my position on the comforter.

The calf's brain guy presses his palm to my pussy.

"Happy Valentine's," he says.

"I'm sorry," I say.

He doesn't say, "For what?"

There is a design going through the calf's brain guy's skin. His forearms are made of damask. It turns inside of him while he fucks me. I hold him by the wrists. He tells me he's going to come. I don't squeeze him. I don't say, "Fuck me some more," in order to keep the hallucination from stopping.

The Sheikh blindfolded me and told me how many steps it was from the floor to the bed. He led my hand. But when he came I saw him. I saw his shitty apartment. I saw the wheezy air conditioner. I saw most of all the palm-tree wallpaper ringing his head. I open my eyes and look at the shimmering wallpaper of the Pierre. I think I will never see palm trees again like it's a discontinued design.

The calf's brain guy has champagne. I take off his coat for him.

"Check-out's tomorrow," he says.

The cork flies out violently into the curtains. I am surprised even though I saw it coming. Before I turn around I set my expression.

"I don't think it's really been a month," I say.

"Close enough."

The calf's brain guy is somewhere behind me doing things to me but I am not with him. Either a month is an arbitrary measurement or it's not. A year is not an arbitrary measurement if I'm really not the same.

He stays with me again. All night I hide my face in his chest, which is soft.

22

The calf's brain guy throws my phone on the bed. I leave his satin tights on the carpet. I feel dread.

On Fifth Avenue there are people ceaselessly. I can't possibly look at each face. The entrance to the Pierre is heated. In the summer it's cooled, but just that square of sidewalk. Outside its boundaries it's me for myself. The calf's brain guy takes me by the shoulders and kisses me on the forehead.

"You're an amazing person," he says.

I buy cigarettes in the first store I see. I buy a beer and drink it out of a paper bag. I walk downtown by myself.

"Now you're just flirting with me," I say.

The delivery guy shrugs.

When my phone's fully charged it shudders forever. I snort a bag of SWEET PUSSY and wait a few minutes until I can't feel. I read the curious, confused, mean, desperate, apologetic texts on my phone like a book.

The art is burned or shot through with arrows or made with scissors and distemper. I stand in front of a white feather sculpture with a motor in it. In a timed way it trembles. I spiral down the Guggenheim with the art guy. The whole time we've been going the wrong way. At the bottom I read what's painted on the wall and it says what we will see is not nihilism but the pure possibility that rises from destruction. I scoff. The art guy has two fingers inside of me.

"I feel so good," he says.

"This show is naïve either way," I say.

I make my dimples show.

"Did you miss me?" I say.

At the cop bar the ex-Ranger does not stand up. I throw my arms around his neck.

"I missed you so much," I say.

I feel him keeping himself away like he doesn't want to touch me but then he does.

I smooth the ex-Ranger's smooth face. We are drunk. There are double and triple versions of us.

"How many other girls did you have up here while I was gone?"

He counts on his fuzzy fingers.

"Four."

I bite him in a fake way.

I wake up and his hands are around my neck. They're not squeezing, they're just there. My shoulders are pinned by his knees. I reach up as much as I can and caress the tops of the ex-Ranger's feet.

"Baby," I say.

The Sheikh told me he was for hire like me.

"Sunni, Shia, I don't care," he said.

"So you make bombs for Jews and Christians, too," I said.

He shrugged.

"If I lived in Israel or Lebanon, why not? I would adapt to my surroundings."

I remember looking out the window at the pastel sky of Dubai.

"I want to buy you a steak."

I look at the guy who buys me things. Then I look at my wrists. I look at the gap between my thighs. If I get too skinny he will leave.

"Rare," I say.

"Did I do something wrong?" he says.

I touch him immediately.

"Not at all."

When the ribeye comes I try to eat it all for him.

After the junk-bond guy comes in my mouth I lay my head on his chest. He pushes his hand down the back of my tights and cups my ass, one of his fingers in the crack.

"I'm right where I'm supposed to be," I say.

He hugs me tighter and doesn't let up. He smells like wool and I fall asleep to the sound of the movie's gunfights.

They all stayed. Because two weeks is not a month, I think. But also because, in the beginning, I didn't pick them. They picked me. Probably my stash of spoons is in the kitchen but it is so hard to get up.

23

"Aren't you happy we're eating cod sperm again?"

At the omakase bar I drape my thigh over the calf's brain guy's. The fish come is much richer in my mouth than his.

"If I wanted to break one of your bones, like a little one, how much would that cost?"

I look at the side of his face. I'm mismanaging him.

"Like a finger?"

He looks at me, too.

"Yeah."

I move my leg.

"Let me think about it," I say.

The bar is striped in an insane way, like a dazzle ship, which is camouflage that is meant to confuse not conceal. The art guy is talking. The bartender is talking. I can hear them but it's getting hard to see.

"How much you think he got paid to paint this?" the art guy says.

"Bank," the bartender says.

I feel for the art guy's knee.

"I need to go to the bathroom," I say.

He passes the coke under his fingers. In the hotel hallway I have a slit of vision that's closing. The exit sign swims at me. When I get outside I'm blind. The cold air is shocking. I squat to my feet. I haven't had a panic attack in such a long time. I listen to the neutral gray hum of Eleventh Avenue. I think I'm supposed to be the one who is dazzling.

I see her back as soon as I walk into the locker room. I find it insulting, like the delivery guy's psychological stamps. She turns to me and her TODAY folds away. I walk back out. Today I don't feel like working out.

I couldn't decide. I put a spicy tuna and a salmon on the Duane Reade counter. The cashier shakes her head.

"I'm not scared of death," I say.

"You should be," she says.

She holds her hand out flat to me and looks the other way. I'm joking. I think about it all the time. I think today a man could kill me. Like everyone, I want to control the way I die.

The ex-Ranger takes me to a restaurant in Queens that has valet parking. I pick at my fish.

"How is it?" he says.

It doesn't matter where he takes me or how it tastes. He could take me anywhere and feed me anything.

"Bony," I say.

I try to instigate a fight.

"Everything about you irritates me."

"Jesus Christ," he says.

He's sitting on the futon. I'm standing in front of him. I jam my high heel into the ex-Ranger's knee.

"I'm expensive," I say.

He kisses my leg.

The guy who buys me things is talking about me to the salesguy. The salesguy is wearing neon bike shorts and his legs are hairless and thick. I'm a little away from them, on a high floor of the Dover Street Market, in a six-thousand-dollar dress.

"You should buy that for her," the salesguy says.

"I don't know if she deserves it," the guy who buys me things says.

Both of them snicker.

"Is your father alive?" the junk-bond guy says.

I look at him like I'm surprised. At one point they all have a theory. There are three or four to choose from.

"Of course," I say.

I don't know if that's true or not. The junk-bond guy puts on my boots for me. I laugh at him. He zips them up.

"There you go, baby," he says.

As a little girl I asked my mother where my father was and she said he didn't care about us. When I was a teenager I thought who he didn't care about was her. I looked for him. I found him.

I have always been suspicious of theories. In a diagram a tangle of lines connects this to that but it doesn't explain why. I try to study my ceiling to make sure it didn't change shape while I was away. But I'm nodding and I can't.

I'm really high. I probably shouldn't have left my apartment. All words blur into symbols.

"Salaam," I say.

"Salaam."

I'm struggling with my money. The bodega guy puts his hand on mine. He takes a ten and four ones and in their place he puts a pack of Marlboro Reds.

"You need matches?" he says.

I shake my head.

24

Two girls work on me. I get elaborate nails that take hours because I have time to waste. Every finger is a different sugar skull.

The calf's brain guy opens my palm and kisses my hand.

I look at my finger and it makes me dizzy. It's purple and throbbing. An ER nurse holds it in the palm of her hand.

"What happened?" she says.

"I don't know," I say.

"Come on, your fucked-up finger is amazing."

My jaw is compulsive. My brain is artificially happy. I snort his line, too.

"Okay. No face."

"No face," he says.

The art guy gets down on his knees. I'm wearing magenta fishnets and I shove my two hands down the front and as soon as he takes the picture I smile really big where he can't see.

I'm on my fourth or fifth Cherry Bomb when the ex-Ranger buzzes in. As soon as he sits down I put my hand on top of his.

"Hey," I say.

He looks at my splint.

"Hey," he says.

He doesn't say anything else.

"Hey," I say.

I'm on Second Avenue when I see the Polish magazine seller. I stop in front of him.

"What are you doing over here? You're supposed to be on Sixth Avenue," I say.

"The police," he says.

When he looks up he recognizes me. He takes off his hood and shows me his horrible nose. He picks up the magazine I was looking at months ago. It is neither less dusty nor more. Like TODAY and SWEET PUSSY I know he has nothing to do with me. I'm making mistakes of perception.

"Three dollars for you."

"Get away from me."

I have the Polish diner deliver because I can't stand to see that woman right now.

Everything exists, in every iteration, so naturally if I look for something I find it. I shift my focus and there it is.

"I want you to cover my eyes because I shouldn't be allowed to see you when you come in me," I text GBT.

While he fucks me the guy who buys me things clamps his hand over my face. He is literal. When he comes naturally I see nothing.

"Did you know Uzbekistan is a doubly landlocked country? All of its neighbors are also landlocked and none of its rivers flow into the ocean."

"I did not know that," the junk-bond guy says.

We're eating Thai food in his living room. What I'm eating is two orders of spring rolls.

"A closed system," he says.

"Like Amex," I say.

He knows this. It makes him happy. He holds one shumai up on his fork and I eat it.

"How do you know that?"

"I know a lot of things," I say.

I was with an Uzbek girl in a bathroom doing coke. She told me that. She also told me she was Miss Uzbekistan at a Miss World pageant on Hainan Island.

"Really?" I said.

"I thought I was going to do something with my life. Then nothing happened."

Her English was good. This was at one of the Saudi's parties and the next day it hurt to walk.

In a closed system nothing is created or destroyed, so every iteration exists always and what it does is change form. That's a justifying explanation. There are still wholesale kitchen supply stores on the lowest Bowery. On what feels like a whim I buy mercury candy thermometers in one of them. There are chandelier stores, too. Showy glass chandeliers, dripping low from the ceilings, almost sitting on the cushions of jewel-tone love seats. I could decorate my apartment. A saleslady comes up to me. She whispers under her breath.

"You are Polish," she says.

"No," I say.

The walls are mirrored and I know that I belong here, matching everything.

25

I walk in the dark and the city is white and quiet. It's a slow blizzard. Somewhere on Fifty-Second Street I see another person. A strong memory of mine is feeling trapped in Manhattan.

I was twelve. It was the first warm day after four brutal months and I walked down Avenue B, all arms and all legs, and suddenly I had this power. Since then it hasn't stopped.

This yoga teacher keeps us in the fetal position forever. I imagine how we must look to her: like evenly spaced, curled-up animals with whom she can do anything. I think she is intoxicated by herself. The TODAY girl is on the next mat. She is wearing a sports bra that cuts her tattoo in two. My eyes are supposed to be closed but they are not.

It could be any time but in here it's dark and pounding.
"When's your birthday?"
"Why?"
I try to put my tongue back in the calf's brain guy's mouth.

"What do you mean, why?" the calf's brain guy says.

"I'm a Cancer," I say.

The art guy takes me to a movie in the basement of MoMA. There are great stretches of boredom. I don't tell him it's the kind of movie I like. I think I should touch his dick but when I look over he is sleeping. It's not his birthday. Birthdays are for wives and real girlfriends, too. The movie's Italian and after two hours there is a massacre.

I sneer at the text that I sent ER: "Want to do something fun."

They can't give Coney Island new teeth. It's still the seediest beach. There is patchy snow on the sand. No one is here. Behind us are projects. In front of us is ocean. I drink a shot of vodka and pass the bottle to him.

"You don't love me," I say.

I touch his knee with my splinted hand.

"I love you," the ex-Ranger says.

We have drunk sex that feels like magic, in an arched alcove of that abandoned building on the boardwalk. These small bursts of joy are supposed to keep people breathing.

I look at the ass of the guy who buys me things and notice it is whiter than the rest of him. I remember that over Christmas he went on a tropical vacation.

"How was the island?"

He's on his hands and knees on top of me.

"What?" he says.

I'm stalling. I don't feel like licking him. When I found my father I asked him to tell me a nice thing about my mother. He said she was the most brilliant person he had met, she was sparkling, and then it went nowhere.

"My asshole. Now," the guy who buys me things says.

I stick my tongue in him as he fucks my tits.

The junk-bond guy fucks me in the guest bedroom. He makes a show of being generous. He tells me to touch myself until I come. Afterward we lie on top of the covers.

"Did this used to be your daughter's room?"

"I have a son," he says.

I can feel him anticipating that I will say something else. When I don't he touches my broken finger carefully.

"I'm nice to you, right?"

I look at him.

"Yes. Thank you," I say.

The first man I ever had sex with was British. He didn't pay me but it was an exchange. He was a manager of a club I wanted to get into. It was so important to me but I can't remember its name. It was on Bleecker and Thompson. I lied and told him I was fourteen. On the Internet I search for it. It was called Life. I shut my computer.

26

The wax lady looks at my vagina and shakes her head.

"I didn't do this," she says.

"Last time I had to go to someone else."

She puts her hand on her white hip. She stares at me silently.

"She was not discreet," I say.

The tiny pinch of the tweezers is so much worse than the wax's wide yank.

"Ingrown," she says.

I think there is come in my eye. It's red. Imagining sperm swimming around my iris makes me squirmy. I can't look at myself. I put my compact away.

"Something in your eye?" the calf's brain guy says.

"You," I say.

He laughs. I steal the olives from his martini. This restaurant only has one bathroom and while he was jerking off on my face somebody was knocking on the door.

"A real boss would fuck me in his corner office during work hours."

He snatches the toothpick back.

"I'll fuck you wherever I want," he says.

I look at the sleeping hermaphrodite. One side is long hair and a tight ass, the other side is breasts and a penis. The Saudi had one of these statues in his garden. This one is iridescent, new, awake. I turn and face the art guy and cross my arms over my chest.

"If I had a dick I'd fuck you in the ass with it. I'd make you suck me off in the stairwell and then I'd come all over your face."

A woman moves away from us.

"But you don't," he says.

The stairwell is lit neon green. It's the color of future vomit. It's screeching with Guantánamo Bay torture music. Actually he came in my mouth. When he said to meet him at the New Museum, first I went to Broadway where it used to be and I felt lost, left behind, like the city no longer wants me.

"You have the sweetest pussy in New York City."

The art guy hip-checks me. I check him back.

The repetition of words and images will not sucker me into thinking there is a pattern when there isn't. The city does not want or not want. It does not trick. The bricks now are stamped IED.

"Why did you get kicked out of the army?"

The ex-Ranger rolls up a twenty.

"I didn't."

"Okay," I say.

I think about teaching the ex-Ranger my system. When I get up to nine bags a day I taper for two weeks until I get back to three. The right way to do heroin is the management of tolerance. I think about confiding in him. He's not the Sheikh. He can't teach me anything. I don't.

The Sheikh only had a hot plate. I stood beside him while he made us something.

"Four threads saffron, it's very important. Are you listening?" he said.

"Yes," I said.

I think they won't have it and then I won't be able to make it. But there they are: thin, handsome saffron threads coiled around inside a glass jar.

"Fucking Whole Foods," I say.

The guy stocking the shelves looks at me knowingly.

"There's no way you have rose water," I say.

"Baking aisle," he says.

I make the khabeesa on my real stove. I make too much, enough for two people, and then I can't eat it. Ice drops out of the sky all day.

I get on top of the desk of the guy who buys me things. I crawl a little and then I look at him. He snaps his fingers at me.

"Bathroom."

"You are zero fun," I say.

He brought me back here without me asking again. I think he is pleased with me. With him I am doing everything right.

"Come here," the junk-bond guy says.

The master bedroom is at the end of the hall and the bed is bigger and whiter than the son's. I sit on it. I lean back on my elbows.

"Is this weird?"

"Come here," I say.

Him too, he is pleased.

I found my tone as a whore almost immediately. It was instinct. It is false submission. Instead of shopping for what I need I let the guy at the MAC store do my makeup.

"Do you bake?" he says.

I let this go. He means my face, floured with setting powder to lock it in place. That Whole Foods is just next door is of no consequence.

"I do everything," I say.

I let him do whatever he wants. He glues on the most extreme faux lashes. He's giddy.

"Girl," he says.

On the train a little girl stares at me with her lips parted. I can't decide whether to smile. I do.

27

The bartender is burning a piece of wood and catching the smoke under a whiskey tumbler.

"I'm a partner," the calf's brain guy says.

I look at him.

"My bonus was six million and it wasn't enough," he says.

Neither the bartender nor I make any sound. I squeeze the calf's brain guy's knee.

"Thank you for telling me that, baby."

The bartender pours our drinks into two smoky glasses. He presents them with a flourish. He gives me a meaningful look that I hate. I take a sip.

"This drink tastes like lung cancer," I say.

The art guy announces we're going dancing. The second thing he says is that the sound system is crystal.

"Am I going to need ecstasy to enjoy this?"

"Yes," he says.

He tosses a white-powder baggie on his island.

"It's molly. You lick it," he says.

I look at it. A tremor of anger moves through me.

"How much does it cost to buy into your fund?" I say.

The art guy crumples his face like he is irritated.

"One million. Or five if you want my father to return your calls, not me."

But when he says the words that are numbers he has the same smug satisfaction as the calf's brain guy, as any rich man I have ever met.

"You looking to invest, Miss Thing?"

I shrug. I lick my finger and drag it through the molly.

I turn my head and the zombie girl's there. She touches my hair. I lay my face on her tits.

"Louisa," I say.

Ecstasy was for the Saudi's parties.

I had been with the Qatari man for a year and I was rusty. In the bathroom at the Saudi's party I did coke with a Polish girl who looked like me ten years younger. We did a double together and in the morning I was smugly satisfied when the man asked me, not her, to go home with him. My body was just dregs, the ecstasy and coke and heroin trailing out of my system, and I was still so unused to being outside when a few hours later the woman came up to me and I apologized for my blood staining the sidewalk.

I lie facing the ex-Ranger with my head on his chest. We're not asleep. We're awake. We're warm, high, sweating on each other. After the man tried to kill me I thought the Sheikh would hear. I thought he would contact me in some way.

The nail girl doesn't have to skip that finger. It's back to looking unhurt like the other ones. I get spiky EKG lines in crazy pink.

"You want any flat lines?" she says.

She does the sound of death, the hospital-machine sound, and then she laughs.

"The last five," I say.

The new stamp is LIFE SUPPORT. There is a new eel roll at Duane Reade.

"Is this a sign that everything is going to change?"

I say it half-heartedly and the cashier sighs at me.

The guy who buys me things is fucking my face and I gag. I knee him off hard and it's so reflexive it scares me. I look at him. I scramble down the hotel bed to his feet. I leave my face pressed against one until I feel his hand on me. It slides between my ass and into my pussy.

"I'm sorry. I need you," I say.

I make myself sick. I text JBG: "I want your cock in my mouth, gagging me, so I can't speak."

I walk with the junk-bond guy across the Brooklyn Bridge.

"Where is your family from?" he says.

"Here," I say.

"Originally."

"Here."

Under our feet the river has a dirty shine.

"You're a Manhattan Indian."

"Yeah," I say.

"Me too."

As soon as we get to the Brooklyn side we turn and head back the way we came. I can see the city so clearly. It's crystal. It does touch me, as it is and not as it was. Of course it does.

28

Not to be cold is the easiest pleasure. The weather is manipulative. I walk across Fourteenth Street wearing that leather jacket that will last me forever with its fringe bouncing off my butt.

In the locker room I peek into every alcove looking for the TODAY girl. I squat down to see the feet in the showers.

"You lost something?" the cleaning lady says.

"Maybe," I say.

This trash restaurant must be a joke. It's a pop-up. I tell our waitress recycled food sounds like a euphemism for puke and I know she wants to agree with me.

"It's about the luxury of waste," the waitress says.

I kick the calf's brain guy and he grabs me by the calf. When our drinks come he holds his up.

"To the luxury of waste," he says.

"To you and me," I say.

I eat an unlaid egg. He eats a fish's fried collar.

"What are we doing here?"

"I just get bored with everything," the calf's brain guy says.

I sit back in my seat and narrow my eyes and smirk at him.

I am creative in the bathroom of the trash restaurant.

"That was inspired, what you were doing to my dick," the calf's brain guy says.

He's pissing in the toilet. Now I smirk at his back, my anxiety eased.

We have to wear paper slippers over our shoes so we don't smudge the infinity room. It is made of mirrors with a maze that ends in a chamber. In math there is the idea of infinity. I look at the art guy and me, multiplied, on all four sides, and above our heads and below our feet. The trick is LED bulbs. This room is finite like everything.

"I'd like to have a thousand of you," the art guy says.

"What a hell that would be," I say.

I jam my pointy elbow into a point on the back of the ex-Ranger.

"God, yes," he says.

"Don't you wish you could do this to your brain?"

"Yes."

With my other hand I drink my Cherry Bomb. The ex-Ranger's head is in his hands. He gets the same tricks as the others. A thing rich men have taught me is that it either has to be prohibitively expensive or it has to be free.

I pin down each of his shoulders with each of my knees. I put my hands on either side of his head.

"You live in a room inside my brain," I say.

He closes his eyes. He opens them and spits in my face.

I found the sound of the call to prayer menacing. I met the Sheikh and I found the sound beautiful. He disappeared and I found the sound indifferent to me.

I buy a street kid another drink. He's drinking Cherry Bombs like me. I tell him I used to live in Dubai.

"How much did cigarettes cost?"

I'm pleased by his relevant question.

"Ten dirhams or three dollars," I say.

He whistles.

"Isn't it oppressive that everything has to have a reason?" I say.

I fold my elbows on the bar and smile at him.

"Are you about to say something about God?"

I shake my head.

There will be nothing left to see it, there will be nothing but nitrogen ice, but it will be gorgeous. The swelling sun will boil off the oceans and blow gas into the sky that will be lush and sunset-colored: pink and gold and orange. I stare at my stained ceiling.

On my knees I mimic the waiter from lunch.

"Sparkling, sir? And for the lady no water at all?"

The guy who buys me things laughs. I think there is nothing wrong with that restaurant either, in the Time Warner Center, like there is nothing wrong with this office with its view of the East River. In my life I have choices. Everything is going fine.

"Suck my cock," he says.

For the junk-bond guy I jump up and down in the middle of his big white bed. The Saudi himself bought me my tits. They're pretty Bs. At any time one could burst and kill me from the inside and that would save other people pain, like his wife who also sleeps in this bed.

"Sit on it," the junk-bond guy says.

29

There is a planet in such permanent winter that its atmosphere has frozen and fallen to the ground.

"There is a planet covered in creatures who do not accept that they will die. They are constantly surprised."

The Sheikh laughed. I was so pleased to please him.

I present my ass to the dermatologist's nurse.

"Do you do this to yourself all the time?" I say.

"It's the only way I keep going," she says.

I nod at her. She shoots me up with B_{12}.

I snap at the calf's brain guy.

"Stop being paternal. It's weird," I say.

He lets go of the door so it shuts in my face. I immediately want to get high.

MON: CLOSED
TUES: CLOSED
WEDS: CLOSED

THUR: CLOSED

FRI: CLOSED

SAT: CLOSED

SUN: CLOSED

"If I had a store those would be the hours."

The art guy laughs and holds my hand.

"I thought you were always open," he says.

In the glass of the painting I look at us and I am shining so bright it's like he's not there. I despise everything about me. I fix my hair.

At Whole Foods I'm in a checkout line with everything I need to make lasagna. I abandon my cart and just leave.

I wear my six-thousand-dollar dress to the cop bar. The ex-Ranger's not even there. One of the gray drunks wants to dance with me.

"You don't get to touch me," I say.

He touches my bare arm. I throw my Cherry Bomb in his face.

Right now if I asked the ex-Ranger any question I think he would answer. He's lying on my back with his dick still in me.

"What else is in that closet?" I say.

All his guns and ammunition are laid out on a bedsheet.

"Is it weird you have a gas mask?"

He picks up a pair of brass knuckles. He gets down on one knee. He takes my hand. I switch with him.

"It's the left hand," I say.

He slips the knuckles on and they fall off. They nearly dent the floor between us.

"Is that a silencer?"

In the middle of a Romanian movie I think I have seen before I close my eyes and when I come to I can't decide if the scene has changed or if my computer was stuck and spinning the whole time and it only woke up when I did.

"Viorel," the man says.

That's his name. When a man says his name it is important that I remember it. It's good for my livelihood. I think about my real name.

"Viorel," I say.

"Would you say you're a venal man?"

"I don't really know what that means."

"Look it up on your phone."

The guy who buys me things doesn't.

"I would say you're a venal woman," he says.

We're stuck in traffic. He already came. It's that drowsy, piss-colored afternoon light in New York.

"Would you say money is the most important thing in the world?"

"Yes," I say.

"This place has really gone downhill," the junk-bond guy says.

I spin our lazy Susan. I keep looking around for the dessert-cart lady because I want an egg custard that will only be texture, no taste. We're on the sixth floor of a dim-sum parlor on East Broadway and the carpet is crunchy and I feel safe. The junk-bond guy sticks his fork in the gelatinous brown sauce of the clams. It stands straight up.

"It's exactly the same," I say.

I can walk for blocks and blocks. I'm fucked-up and it feels like float-ing. It rains for three days and then it commits to mildness. I throw my puffy coat in a trash can.

30

I buy an iced coffee and walk around drinking it. I walk up to the Home Depot on Twenty-Third Street. I buy nails and paint. I'm going to paint my ceiling. At Forever 21 I buy five pairs of white panties.

One by one I put on the panties and take a picture of my butt. Via text message I distribute the photos evenly.

The calf's brain guy fucks me through a hole he's ripped in the crotch of my panties. I lie flat on my stomach with my skirt flipped up. I twist my fingers with his. I hold his hands for a long time. We're at the Pierre again.

"Are you sad?" I say.

"No," he says.

The past is a pattern but trying to re-create it is an echo. I could tell him but he wouldn't listen like I wouldn't listen.

The enormous canvas looks like the proofs of every page of a long book unbroken by chapters or paragraphs. And when I get close I see the sentences aren't sentences and the words aren't words and the letters aren't letters but stylized black scribbles.

"I like this," the art guy says.

"It's a nightmare," I say.

I feel unsettled all the way to the deepest part of me.

"Will you control her?" the bartender says.

I sit down next to the ex-Ranger.

"Control me," I say.

The bartender is already making a Cherry Bomb. The ex-Ranger looks at us, confused.

"I don't know what you're talking about," the ex-Ranger says.

"I threw my drink on a drunk last week."

Everything doesn't have to be a secret. I touch him.

"I want to make out with you in the ladies' bathroom."

"Me too," he says.

This yoga teacher touches but not everyone. I think she must decide by class performance. I perform very well. I lie on the floor and anxiously wait for her. I smell her stop. She is preceded by the smell of lavender. She rubs her hands above me. She presses my shoulders down and holds them there. As soon as she leaves they pop back up.

I go into the Strand because I want a book. I buy a suicidal poet. By its nature the end of everything will have a meaning. It will stop chaos. I want confirmation.

The delivery guy has shed his sweatshirt and his T-shirt says THAT OLD COKE MAGIC under a photograph of Magic Johnson in a full fur.

"I like your outfit," I say.

The delivery guy peeks under my arm.

"Usually I get to come in," he says.

I shut the door in his face.

"You don't want to come in, do you?"

The delivery guy for the Polish diner looks at me quizzically.

"I know," I say.

I'm drinking with the guy who buys me things. He buys us both Bushmills and I think I know nothing about him.

"Are you a Protestant?" I say.

He laughs.

"I'm not anything. Are you anything?"

"No," I say.

The junk-bond guy is upstate for the week, not just the weekend. In a show that is about time there are over thirty years of nine hundred telegrams that say I AM STILL ALIVE and one that says I AM NOT GOING TO COMMIT SUICIDE DON'T WORRY. I am at the Guggenheim by myself.

When the plane lifted off it banked and then left the Gulf behind and I thought: I am doing the right thing. Passport control at JFK was the most familiar chaos.

"Welcome home," the man said.

I know he says that to every citizen. He stamped me in.

31

I'm walking on Avenue A when a cuff falls off my arm and goes spinning down the street. I need to eat.

I get frozen yogurt at Walgreens. I wander around the store and eat it. The guard starts to follow me. I look over my shoulder. I know I have to pay.

"Don't worry," I say.

I put a ten down.

"You're a beautiful woman so you always get what you want?"

"God," I say.

I throw down another five on the bodega counter.

The calf's brain guy takes me to the restaurant in the Time Warner Center but for dinner. He orders all the supplements: caviar, foie gras, Wagyu. I calculate the bill in my head. I feel pressured.

"Do you want to go to the bathroom with me?"

"I want one year," the calf's brain guy says.

I glare across the room at the different waiter.

"You've never even shown me your office," I say.

The art guy wants to film us fucking. I humor him.

"What will you be wearing?" I say.

"For one thing."

He holds me by the shoulders and looks at me intently.

"Very limited-edition sneakers," he says.

"Absolutely not."

The ex-Ranger's started shooting up. He squats down on his haunches like a villager. One thing about him for which I am grateful is that he never talks about Afghanistan. I never talk about Dubai. I don't bring it up again, the right way to do heroin.

These bricks are called RIHANNA. I lick a bag affectionately. I look around my apartment at what I will need to put away before I let the delivery guy in.

I look at Stuyvesant Town from the street. I don't go in. We couldn't have air conditioners until they rewired all the buildings when I was nine or ten. We had Hunter fans, all other fans were shit. When the buzzer was busted my mother threw the key out the window in a red felt baggie that had come with a piece of jewelry. I look up at our window with the Friedrich AC sticking out that is now only hers.

It's not spring enough for rooftops. I slide off the lap of the guy who buys me things.

"This heat lamp's warmer than you."

He's preoccupied.

"If I go to the bathroom and don't come back it means I saw somebody I know. I'll text you where to meet."

"If I have to wait more than an hour you forfeit the date. I get my full rate either way."

"I know the terms," he says.

I look up. I can't see a single star because New York City has its own glow that obscures all others. Anyway, their light is from ten or a thousand years ago. Right now the Empire State Building is the brightest thing I see and I greatly prefer it. He gets up.

I play with the junk-bond guy's cock. I twirl the tip of my tongue around the flare like it's an ice-cream cone. We're at the movies and he moans audibly but I never get caught.

"You go over there you don't get to call me for help, not even once," my mother said.

It was the day after my eighteenth birthday. It was hot. I was standing in front of the air conditioner so it blew up the back of my flimsy top.

"I know the terms," I said.

The nail girl paints her own finger while my hand sets in a UV dryer.

"This thing gives you cancer," I say.

"Skin cancer."

My nails are gold teeth.

32

I put my wineglass down and it just shatters. Glass flies everywhere, in our steaks. I clamp my hand on top of his.

"Don't eat that," I say.

In his eyes there is a rush of feeling.

"Don't eat yours," the calf's brain guy says.

The art guy recounts the entire plot of a movie he saw recently. Now I want to talk.

"I just saw this movie that was only blue screen. The filmmaker was going blind from AIDS. You could hear him but all you could see was blue. He said this thing about his mind being fine but his body dying. He said it was like a naked lightbulb in a dark, ruined room. I'm the opposite of that. My body is a naked lightbulb and my mind is a dark room."

I sniff coke drip up my nose. So does he. I can't believe I said that out loud. I look at him with trepidation.

"Your body is everything," he says.

I'm lying on top of the ex-Ranger and he's looking at me in a way that's making me uncomfortable.

"Let's go get a drink," I say.

"What if I asked you to stop?" he says.

"Let's go get a drink."

I look to my right and watch myself make cat and cow in the side mirror. Mostly I watch the clock. Forty more minutes, thirty more minutes, twenty more minutes, ten more minutes: it's always ticking down and then yoga will be over. I never just walk out.

I sit on the couch with the ex-Ranger's Glock in my hand. I have screwed the silencer to the muzzle. I think how I would be found by smell. My body two weeks rotted into the upholstery but still unmistakably mine, my teeth. At the end I don't want there to be anything left of me. I would never kill myself like this.

The wax lady smiles at my pussy.

"Very nice. How's everything?" she says.

"Very nice," I say.

The guy who buys me things wants to buy me for the weekend. He wants to drive me out to Montauk. I'm superstitious about leaving the city, like I won't get back in.

"What if you murder me and dump my body in the marsh?"

It's teatime in the powder-blue restaurant at Bergdorf's. I down my champagne. He eats a scone.

"I promise not to," he says.

I tap one of his gold teeth with one of my gold-teeth nails.

"What?" the junk-bond guy says.

I shake my head.

"I just wanted to do that."

I watched from his bed.

"What does that do?" I said.

"It conducts electricity."

The Sheikh turned over his shoulder to look at me. He was wearing latex gloves.

"It's very important," he said.

A plane hovering just under the cloud cover is not enough. Australian salt fields will still look like blue stained glass. The Amazon River will still look like a curly muddy snake with a head somewhere and also a tail. It is best to see life satellite-like, with altitude. I let the MAC guy put gold lipstick on my mouth. He leans back and looks at me.

"You thought you was fierce," he says.

I try to see myself but it's hard to focus. I'm up to nine bags. I hold up my shaky nails to my lips. He snaps in my face.

"Slay," he says.

33

The blue woman sits down at my table. She has blintzes.

"You're too skinny," she says.

I'm already having hot-pink borscht.

"I don't want to have to pay for this."

"My God, it's on the house."

I take a bite while she watches me. They're cherry.

"Thank you," I say.

I have that sensation sometimes of waking up and not knowing where I am except that I'm not asleep. It's the calf's brain guy who grabs my face and kisses me hard on the street.

In a hot white tent on Randall's Island, at an art fair, there are close-up photos of tongues with all their problems written on them in ink, like scallops, cracks, and spleen deficiencies. The white card says IT's SYMPTOMATIC.

"I'm afraid to look at my tongue now," I say.

"What do you have to be worried about, baby? I'm the one who let ten million walk out the door yesterday."

I look at the art guy, concerned. This is the second time he's brought this up.

"Are you going to get fired?"

"I'm his son. He can't fire me."

I stick out my tongue at him. He sticks out his tongue at me. It's fat and pink.

In the middle of the East River, on a ferry, I smile at the art guy and he puts his arm around me.

I run my tongue over his lips.

"I lost my job," the ex-Ranger says.

"When?" I say.

"Like two months ago."

I'm not surprised. I put my face in his neck and smell his skin. I think probably I won't see that bad suit again.

"Fuck Bank of America," I say.

Before I go I leave all the cash I have on me in his bathroom.

I took off the lid of one of the pressure cookers on his tarp. I looked inside.

"Does it bother you? What I do for a living?"

"No," I said.

The Sheikh crossed his arms. He smirked.

"Violence is random unless you're the violent one," I said.

I smirked at him. I put the lid back on.

I put a tube of lube and an eel roll on the Duane Reade counter. The cashier looks at me.

"You seem like an interesting person," he says.

I laugh.

At the movies I sit in the junk-bond guy's lap and cross my feet up on a seat in front of us. I tuck my head under his chin. I watch the black curtains and not the screen.

"You're a sweet girl," he says.

It did bother me. It bothered me that the Sheikh sold his bombs to the Saudi and then he had no idea where they went. He lost control.

This Belgian prostitute movie is nearly without story and yet there are mundane discrepancies, meant to telegraph an unraveling, until at the climax she comes and murders a client with scissors. I roll my eyes at my computer.

I meet the guy who buys me things in the lobby of the Pierre.

"Happy weekend," I say.

"Happy weekend," he says.

In the elaborate robot corset he bought me I crawl to him. I look at how his socks correspond with the carpet. They're both diamonds. If they were hexagons it could mean I was in the same room as before, with the calf's brain guy, and that would truly worry me. While I'm waiting I sway my ass back and forth, almost imperceptibly.

"Do it again," he says.

I slink back the way I came.

"Let's go out," he says.

"Why?" I say.

I'm surprised. He sticks his foot out.

"Tie my shoes."

Barneys is around the corner. I sit inside a glass cube. The guy who buys me things holds one arm and the salesguy holds the other and they stand me up in the most fragile silver heels.

"So she can't run away from me," the guy who buys me things says.

I'm just inside a different repetition, his and mine. I know how it goes. I'm not concerned.

"Exactly," I say.

The salesguy giggles in a squirmy way.

I look at my squid.

"I believe in reason, too."

"Good," the guy who buys me things says.

I look at him. He winks at me and drinks his Protestant whiskey.

"What happened in the world of wealth management this week?"

"The wealthy got wealthier," he says.

"You're a partner, right?" I say.

He snorts.

"You've seen my office."

He bought us tickets to the ballet. During Act II, when Giselle is among the dead girls who dance men to death, the prima ballerina falls out of her zigzag jumps and cracks her ankle gruesomely. I jump like I've been shocked. She lost control in less than a second. His hand is in the slit of my dress and he squeezes me.

I snort my bags in the bathroom with the water running. I believe reason makes patterns more beautiful than ballet. The scissors in my makeup bag are tiny and pink. I look at them and laugh. I emerge naked though fully groomed.

"Let's walk in the park," he says.

"Why not," I say.

We lie in the Sheep Meadow in Central Park on a Sunday afternoon on a blanket he bought.

"I want to fuck you in the sun," he says.

I trace my fingernail up his open palm.

"How much did you get for your bonus this year?"

He looks at me like he's been waiting for this question. His voice in my ear is a hoarse, bossy whisper.

"Three million dollars," the guy who buys me things says.

For dinner we have room service and airplane bottles from the mini-bar. He orders lamb shish kebabs. We're slurry.

"Do you only get wet for partners, or VPs, too?"

He slides the stick through his teeth and reminds me of the Saudi. I am different from who I was then. I decide to give a variation on the right answer, a mundane discrepancy, I think.

"VPs too," I say.

"How about associates?" he says.

"Yes."

"Analysts?"

"Yes."

"Some toothless fuck on welfare who lives in his mother's basement?"

I laugh.

"I'm always wet," I say.

The guy who buys me things gets angry. His style is contained.

"If I dumped you in the marsh nobody would look for you," he says.

I eat a French fry and hold his unsteady gaze with mine.

"You promised not to."

———

In the middle of the night I wake up the guy who buys me things. I give him a theatrical blow job. I have a splitting headache.

"Are you happy?" I say.

"I am," he says.

The spice smell of leftover kebabs has settled like a usual fragrance.

34

"Okay, baby."

I stand outside the Pierre's revolving doors and light a cigarette. The entrance is not heated or cooled. It's spring and in between extremes of weather. I think I could send a telegram to somebody that says I AM STILL ALIVE.

"Thank you," I say.

The guy who buys me things kisses me on the cheek and walks away.

The calf's brain guy feeds me bone marrow on a spoon. I want our equilibrium.

"I want you to punch me in the face," I say.

"I don't care what you want," he says.

Under the table I slip out of my shoe and put my foot on his cock.

I stand on his balcony in the dusk and let him film my butt.

"Look at me. Over your shoulder," the art guy says.

I do, slowly. If I'm really not the same I can improvise if I want without changing our rhythm. It's nothing like unraveling.

———

"Okay, you can come in."

He grins all the way in and then he stops.

"Yo," the delivery guy says.

I thoroughly cleaned up. I look where he's looking, at the wall where I've taped up every empty dope bag, almost.

"I was going to send you a telegram the other day," I say.

"I don't think that's a thing anymore."

I put down my Cherry Bomb. I loop my hand in the ex-Ranger's belt and tug him. I think he would look for me.

"You're getting skinny."

He looks at me grimly.

"You know that thing I told you, about the whore in Colombia, that wasn't the most fucked-up thing I've ever seen," he says.

I let go of his belt.

"I know," I say.

I kneed him in the face. It was between my legs. He dropped what he had and I stabbed it into the first part of him I could reach, which was his back. It was a short, sharp knife. Luckily I was still dressed. It was all luck. I limped out the front door and took the elevator to the street, where I bled on the sidewalk until the woman in black gloves helped me. But I still don't know how I got away.

The suicidal poet is romantic, as if he, as he is, will live on in the chaos of the world even after he's dead. Life is decorative and confusing. Death should be clarity. I glance up at my ceiling as if for affirmation.

In the locker room I get so close to the mirror while I'm putting on my eyeliner my nose brushes it. If the TODAY girl is here I refuse to see her, even in the periphery.

In the soft hallways of the office of the guy who buys me things I don't look at any banker and no banker looks at me. At the end of a hall I close the door. I sit across from him like I'm being interviewed, except I drape my legs over the second chair.

"I'm listening if my eyes move. I'm just watching the screens," the guy who buys me things says.

On his desk are two computer monitors and there is a TV on the wall behind my head. It's before four. The market is open.

"I'm not saying anything," I say.

"Crawl under the desk and take off my pants."

The junk-bond guy and I are back at the dim-sum parlor. The dessert-cart lady makes a beeline for me.

"You are my customer, I remember what you like," she says.

The junk-bond guy gives me a pointed look. She is absolutely right that all I want for lunch is egg custards, just texture, no taste. I take four of them and the junk-bond guy passes her a folded-up five.

"Do you miss Bonus Day now that you're retired?" I say.

He smiles at me.

"I got my bonus in hundred-thousand-dollar checks. That was the highest amount payroll could issue. I got a stack of them. Have you ever seen a hundred checks for a hundred thousand dollars?"

"I get paid in cash," I say.

I flutter my fingers over the head of the junk-bond guy's dick and then I mimic what the dessert-cart lady said.

35

Thirty-two girls make four rows of eight in eight columns of four. Over and over they do the same narcotic thing. Eventually there are small, synchronized changes. It looks like an opium dream, like it could go on forever, but of course it doesn't. Again they are all meant to be dead. I bought a single ticket to *La Bayadère*. Ballet is just an excuse for patternmaking. This time nobody fucks up though I wait for it alertly.

I tie a ribbon around my waist so the two tails of the bow slide down the crack of my ass. I text a photo to all five of them.

In the middle of the night the calf's brain guy and I go dancing at the dim-sum parlor.

"Jesus," I say.

All the tables have been cleared away. I look for the dessert-cart lady behind the bar, pouring egg-custard-flavored shots. At least she's not there. He's holding me plastered to his chest.

"I don't know what to do," he says.

Naturally patterns create intersections, I think. The good thing is everyone's smoking. I put a cigarette between my teeth. I feel pacified. I blow smoke away from the calf's brain guy's ear.

"Don't do anything. That's what I would do," I say.

The art guy shows me the film of my butt.

"This is long," I say.

Also it's large. It's projected on his special white wall. I expect him to touch himself but he just sits there. I anticipate the part where I look over my shoulder. I get up and leave the room before I show my face.

I bring a bath towel up to the ex-Ranger's tar paper roof. I lie on it and tan myself. The ex-Ranger comes up through the hatch door. He stands above me.

"How much does it cost to fuck you?"

I'm wearing sunglasses but also I put my hand over my eyes.

"What?" I say.

He starts counting out the hundreds I just left in his bathroom. There's no wind. He doesn't really mean it. The bills fall onto my stomach one by one.

"Keep going," I say.

He fucks me in the sun. He hugs his whole body to mine and drops his head in the crook of my sweating neck. He flips me over to look at me. That I'm in love with him doesn't change anything.

I'm giving the guy who buys me things a hand job in the back of a car and the driver keeps looking in the rearview. I meet his eyes and roll mine and his dart away. He must know rich people do things wherever they want, or he needs to learn.

———

"Your pussy is so warm."

"I'm alive."

The junk-bond guy makes a face above me. I think of how clean I am: my asshole rimmed with soap, my body scrubbed with sugar, my skin slathered in shea butter, my nails filed, my cuticles cut, my pussy stripped, my brows tweezed, my teeth bleached, my hair shined, my perimeter of perfume. Many times I have thought, what am I going to do with this body?

"I can't believe it either," I say.

After the man tried to kill me I still waited for the Sheikh and it felt like it could go on forever but of course it didn't. My residence visa expired and I didn't buy another one. I bought a plane ticket to JFK instead.

My heroin dreams dwindle and end and then I snort three more bags.

36

I tan myself on my own roof. I open my eyes and see an old queen.

"You're not wearing any clothes," he says.

"It's a workday," I say.

"It's Memorial Day."

Summer, I think, like a child, because actually it's three weeks away.

I'm wearing a bombastic white jumpsuit. I pull my hair off my neck and turn around for the calf's brain guy. He punches me. My ears ring.

The art guy has a pool on his roof. He looks at me lecherously from a lounge chair. I look back at him from a pink plastic float.

"How come we never go skinny-dipping?"

"I don't know," he says.

It's a pleasant sensation being suspended like this, weightless above the heavy city. People who think it never ends think this is what it's like: hovering in the air, unmoved by earthly emotions. I laugh to myself. That's not heaven. Heroin's ten dollars a bag.

"What?" the art guy says.

"Nothing," I say.

I kick my foot in the water and the float drifts away.

I kick his shin.

"Look at my eye."

He's sitting on the futon and I'm standing up. He looks at my face. He grabs it by the chin.

"What do you want me to do? You want me to kill him?"

"No," I say.

As soon as the ex-Ranger lets me go I climb in his lap and wrap my arms and legs around him.

At Duane Reade the cashier sucks in all his breath. I'm wearing zero makeup.

"You shouldn't let him do you like that," he says.

"It was an extra grand."

He makes a disgusted face.

"Fuck off," I say.

He refuses to ring me up.

It's monstrous that light ten or a thousand years old is just now reaching people who look up at the stars and make maps and meaning of it. It's like the dancing ghost girls. It's like the suicidal poet living on and on in his pretty words. It's like the light of me will reach another world before this one dies. I wake up in an impossible position. My knees jammed into my face, in the smallest ball, in an inside corner of my couch.

I put my hand on his cock.

"Hey," I say.

I'm a little too high, like I timed it wrong. I close my eyes.

"I just want to close my eyes and let you do things to me," I say.

"You need to take better care of yourself," he says.

I look at the guy who buys me things. My concealer hasn't changed. "You never said anything before."

He shrugs. I put my arms around him and lay my head on his shoulder.

"Sometimes it's scary," I say.

He lays his head on top of mine. We're in the lobby of the Time Warner Center and people stream around.

I pick the shortest line and end up with hot pho. I'm underneath the art guy's apartment, in gas fumes, but I'm not with him. Across the jammed picnic table I smile into the sunglasses of the junk-bond guy.

"Remember last year?"

"I do," I say.

He means last summer, our first date. That was two weeks after I flew into JFK and in three weeks it will be summer again. He bites the head off a fried anchovy.

"Best year of my life," he says.

"Liar."

I think of the burning sun and the best year of mine.

I thought of the burning sun and true happiness and how sad that was. I thought of the Sheikh, who disappeared to marry a virgin his mother picked out. I thought of my mother, who went nowhere, whose brilliance had dimmed and gone out by the time I knew her. I thought of the rich man who paid to fuck me and then tried to kill me. I thought of all the other rich men who paid to fuck me, who had the money to buy a girl too beautiful, too young, too sparkling, like the laws of the universe didn't apply to them, to act like a fantasy and not a person, a thing they could leave on the floor of a hotel room when they got bored like anything else they once had to possess. I thought of how I could be bought. I thought of the whole, overall pattern of my life. I thought of how old I was. August in Dubai, even when I moved from my air-conditioned apartment to an air-conditioned car to an air-conditioned restaurant in an air-conditioned mall, was unbearably hot. All the time I felt suffocated. I made a decision. I would go home and give myself one year.

Every week, every day, every hour, every minute, every second everything is changing. It's dying and it's never coming back. I miss my gold-teeth nails. I look at the foil wrapped around my fingers and mourn them.

37

I bury my face in the neck of the calf's brain guy so we don't have to speak. He squeezes his arms around me tight but I don't feel suffocated. He just wants to injure me in ways that will fade or I can fix, that's who he is, not a killer.

While the art guy is sleeping I creep into his glass living room. I sit on his hard black couch. I look at his camera on its tripod. I get up and take off the lens cap and push the power button and sit down again. I see myself in the viewfinder naked and tiny and all hair. I look into the eye of the camera and I don't say anything.

"Karina?" the art guy says.

"Coming, baby," I say.

I shut it off and hurry back to the bedroom.

With my phone I take a photo of my face. I move into the right light and take another one. Then I delete them.

I put my hands on the ex-Ranger's forehead. I press my thumbs between his eyebrows. He holds me by my upper arms. We're at the cop bar, on two stools, but it feels like we are nowhere and on nothing.

"Sometimes you make me happy," I say.

He giggles his nasty giggle. I imagine us in the future. I see two old junkies bickering on a street in Queens. I giggle my nasty giggle, too.

"Do you want to get a coffee?"

I'm pointing the hair dryer at the TODAY girl like a gun. I put it down.

"No," I say.

This Popsicle is café con leche flavored. I lick it and smoke a cigarette at the same time. Three teenage girls say something mean to me. Later I watch a middle-aged lady salsa in a circle of men. I'm in Tompkins Square Park and the air smells like liquor. Later still I eat a plain slice on a bench beside two white-haired women who are bitching about their mailman, who steals packages, and I almost start crying.

When I was a little girl I was not allowed to go to Tompkins Square. Stuyvesant Town had its own park, as my mother always pointed out, and playgrounds numbered one to twelve. In the center of the Stuy Town Oval was a fountain and on the worst days of winter it would freeze. The falling water would stop in long, solid shapes that bothered me. Because it was stuck in a pattern that was random. That was how it was just because at that second it was cold enough. Also it was freakish, how it had changed states. The ice looked beautiful and mean. I looked at it from a little away until I was no longer bothered but mesmerized. I wasn't allowed to go to Tompkins Square because it was full of junkies, nodding, in their own worlds, who also bothered me.

It was the first drug I ever did. I had never even smoked pot. I walked out of the woods of Stuy Town, down the concrete of Avenue B, all arms and all legs, with ten dollars in my fist. But the man gave it to me for free.

"Taste this. Come back if you like it," he said.

I snort an ISIS bag and I'm jealous of my twelve-year-old self, with all that brand-new power, about to do heroin for the only first time.

After he's come but while he's still sweating all over me I reach back and hold the balls of the guy who buys me things.

"How do you always know what to do?"

"I can read your mind," I say.

He laughs into my collarbone but I'm not joking. I can. All their minds are the same.

The junk-bond guy takes me to an office tower in Midtown, the headquarters of Morgan Stanley. We ride the elevator to a high floor. Everyone there is happy to see him. Though he does not introduce me all of the men speak to me. None of the women do. They give that hurt look like I get on the subway but much deeper. At the end of a hallway the junk-bond guy opens a door.

"This was my office," he says.

I peek inside. I see the river and this time it's the Hudson.

"Look at that view," I say.

For lunch we go around the corner to an overpriced diner. I hold up my surprisingly good martini in a toast.

"Where you used to be king."

38

Somebody tries to open the door and I grab her wrist.

"Don't worry, my love, I keep it locked," she says.

The wax lady rubs me down with vitamin E.

"That's smart," I say.

I was dumb like any eighteen-year-old. This girl told me her friend's sister did it. She said she went over there for one year and made enough money that she wouldn't have to work for five.

"You have to do all the pervert shit, not just fuck them. You have to do whatever they want. Like old men, like with harems."

"I get it," I said.

"They buy you stuff, too, whatever you want," she said.

We were doing coke in the bathroom at a club in Chelsea where we were both bottle girls.

I have to get my hair cut again. I look at the curled-up ends around my chair and resent them. They are naturally nerveless and bloodless and emotionless and it felt like nothing when the scissors cut them. I look at the hairdresser.

"Don't you want a photo for your Instagram?"

"Last time you said no," she says.

I let her take one of the curls falling down my back.

The calf's brain guy is making me come so many times. I'm light-headed. Also we're on a Circle Line cruise and everything is unsteady. Everyone who was at the dim-sum parlor the other night is now here. That's what it feels like. I see my pleasured face in the ship bathroom's scratchy mirror.

"God, stop," I say.

"I have forty million dollars just in the bank. I deserve you," the calf's brain guy says.

A shirtless man wearing a cape that is the American flag makes me a balloon animal on the train.

"It's a rat."

"Thank you," I say.

It's hot pink. I carry it by the tail down the street. When the art guy opens his apartment door I drop it at his feet.

At the bodega a wasted guy starts throwing hundreds on the counter in front of me.

"You need to be wearing a dress, girl, some high-heel shoes. Look at you."

I look at my flip-flops. I push one of the bills toward the bodega guy.

"Let me get a carton," I say.

Back at my apartment I am compelled to get rid of everything I own. I open my closet and look at my beautiful dresses. There are too many prints and colors, all clashing. I pull out every one that is not black, white, or red.

"Here. I brought you something."

I dump out all my empty dope bags onto his futon. He laughs.

"What am I supposed to do with that?" the ex-Ranger says.

I fling my hand around at his blank walls.

"Decorate," I say.

On Park Avenue I smoke a cigarette outside the office of the guy who buys me things. The junk-bond guy's office is over on Broadway. I watch the guy selling Sabrett hot dogs from his street cart. I rub a finger on the extreme tension at the base of one of my eyebrows.

We lie on the white bed stripped to the sheets. Our foreheads are touching and our knees and our feet. I put my hands flat on the junk-bond guy's chest.

"Oh, baby," he says.

He sounds distressed.

"Oh, baby," I say.

Outside it's getting so hot.

39

Our dessert's too lovely. It's meringue, mini violets, and sugared ice.

"I can't eat that."

"For a year I'd pay you a million," the calf's brain guy says.

"That's only one-fortieth of just what you have in your bank account. That's probably less than your interest," I say.

"Okay, two."

I put one of the tiny violets in my mouth but I don't bite it.

I hold onto the balcony railing and look across the East River to the dark park on the Manhattan side. When I was a teenager I was doing this same thing but looking at Brooklyn. The perspective has flipped. The art guy comes in me. Of course I wasn't getting paid either. I had this boyfriend who broke my heart.

"I'm looking for a job," he says.

"Great," I say.

I'm looking at his wall where he's taped up my heroin bags but erratically. The rows are wavy and make no visual sense.

"I've always had to work. My whole life."

He says this in a self-righteous way, like I haven't. On the futon I turn my head to the ex-Ranger. I brush off his shoulder.

"What?"

"Just getting the chip off your shoulder," I say.

There will come a time before the universe ends when each particle will be isolated in its own horizon but that is now. TODAY. I roll my face into a corner of my couch.

We get coffee at the café inside the gym.

"What does your tattoo mean?"

"That it's today. It's never tomorrow or yesterday," the TODAY girl says.

"That's what I thought," I say.

"It's a reminder. When I see my back in the mirror."

I feel slightly sick. We're not in a bathroom. There's only double espresso, no cocaine.

"What do you do?" she says.

I laugh.

"You would like this book," I say.

From my gym bag I give her the suicidal poet.

"How much would it cost to have you all to myself?"

It's not just a coincidence that I'm having this conversation twice in one week. We are at that stage in our relationship, all of us. We are nine months in, thirty-nine weeks. It's natural.

"Give me a number," I say.

"Forty thousand a month plus all expenses," the guy who buys me things says.

I play with his wedding ring.

"I want another martini," I say.

———

The junk-bond guy fucks me in the maid's room on the smoky couch. I think about how troubled he was last week. I curve around to look at him.

"Am I being disciplined?"

He pushes my face forward again.

"Don't talk."

He fucks me so angrily he comes in a second.

I was on the subway without my mother and in the crush before the doors opened a man stuck his hand up my skirt and grabbed my crotch and asked me how much I cost. I was wearing one of my outlandish outfits but in an instant all my confidence disappeared. I knew it was my fault. I had rolled the waist on the skirt, twice. I remember his hoarse, bossy whisper in my ear. I remember it being a new sound. I was ten or eleven.

The window-unit AC is not Friedrich, it's LG. It blows black dust around my apartment. I leave it on, set at sixty, even when I'm gone because I can. On the street it's dark but it's loud. It's really summer now, I think, not like a child.

"Do you want some of them closed?"

I'm getting evil eyes. I look at the nail girl like she's an idiot.

"What good would that do?" I say.

40

At the Polish diner it's only the waitress.

"Where's your mother?" I say.

"In the hospital."

I look at her.

"Beth Israel?"

"We live in Jersey," she says.

The floor of the elevator, not the clams, is what's gelatinous. It's sticky with spilled drinks. It's after hours at the dim-sum parlor and I ash on the carpet. I'm giving the calf's brain guy the cold shoulder.

"I can't go higher than two, come on," he says.

"I don't know anything about you. I can't even picture where you work all day and you want me to give up all my relationships with my other clients," I say.

Then a song comes on and I turn my back to him and float my arms up like the other girls, but better, two beats slower.

The art guy's office is actually on Wall Street.

"Retro," I say.

He sneaks us in at three a.m. We run down a hallway holding

hands and giggling. His father's desk is a mess. He clears a space for me. From up here, on my hands and knees, I can see both rivers. They are the black bands, to the west and the east, between the glittering.

"Put some coke in my asshole."

"I have never been this hard," the art guy says.

"I love your everything."

I look at what I'm wearing, which is monochromatically white. I smile at the cashier.

"Just this," I say.

I'm careful not to give her my evil-eye nails when I hand her the spicy tuna.

I wonder what the laundry lady thinks. Every week lately the only panties are five white pairs, progressively more ripped. But I have my laundry picked up and delivered so I don't know. The dry cleaning I take myself. The dry cleaning lady is holding up a dress.

"We had to run it twice. Something on it we couldn't get off," she says.

She draws her finger down the sides of the long V, the neckline cut all the way to the waist.

"See? When I turn it in the light? What is that?"

It's come.

"No idea," I say.

As an exercise I try to stay away from the ex-Ranger.

"What?" I say.

The ex-Ranger is pretending to be asleep.

"What?" I say.

I straddle him. He won't open his eyes.

"What?" I say.

"Stop it," he says.

He puts his hand flat against my sternum but he doesn't push.

We are spoon-fed what looks like chocolate cake at the end of the show but inside, deceptively, it's tiramisu, which I hate. I open my mouth and spit it out. The guy who buys me things does the same. The actor feeding us looks annoyed.

"Please don't spit on the floor," he says.

"Fifty thousand," the guy who buys me things says.

"I've had a much higher offer," I say.

I watch the guy who buys me things get mad and then control it.

The junk-bond guy leads me by the hand to the master bedroom.

"This is where you belong," he says.

I wonder if he's as exhausted as me, with all the calculations he's been making. I stand on my toes and touch my forehead to his forehead.

"I'm sorry," I say.

"For what?"

I don't say anything.

"It's okay," he says.

"They think money makes them interesting. It's not hard to work that."

He is listening intently to me. He is young and pretty. I look him up and down.

"It used to be easy to steal from Century 21. It probably still is," I say.

The ex-Ranger walks in. I look at NY1 on one of the TVs and it says 9:23 a.m.

"What are you doing here?" I say.

"I'm here all the time, not just Wednesdays. Who's that?" the ex-Ranger says.

I sigh at the street kid. I wanted to unwind. I give the street kid a couple of twenties.

"Go get a manicure," I say.

"You make me feel lawless, like I could take any shape," I say.

The ex-Ranger pushes his fingers into my hair.

"But it's not true," I say.

At first I got hurt. Strangers are rough. I didn't yet understand that it makes all the difference to be loved. I told the Sheikh that.

"That's not love," he said.

I buy a light switch, a cable, a paint roller from the hardware store in my neighborhood. I look at the hardware guy and sigh.

"Do you need a handyman?"

"No," I say.

41

"I don't think Katushka is your real name," the calf's brain guy says.

I eat a piece of rabbit. It's gamey, like I'm really eating another mammal, and I feel my true human nature, which is barbaric survival at all costs. I feel grossed out.

"What is it?" he says.

"Whatever you want it to be, baby."

"I don't know anything about you either."

The art guy taps the coke guy's limousine business card on his island.

"I can't pay you both," he says.

I look at the scraped vial in disbelief. Immediately I start recalculating.

"You got fired. He saw the security tape of his desk," I say.

"No. I'm just going on a trip in a few weeks and I need to keep my expenses down," the art guy says.

I pick up my purse that I just put down.

"I don't know why I even bother with you," I say.

The city is expressing its musk. Urine is still its base. Between the sidewalks the points of my heels stick in the tar like the animal blood after

Eid. In Dubai it was supposed to be illegal to slaughter at home. It grossed out the expats like me. It was only lawful to use abattoirs. But still it was a Muslim country. I want to climb out of my skin and leave it on the street.

The delivery guy sits on the couch next to me.

"What's your interest in the Middle East?" I say.

"It's just where the fucked-up shit's going down right now. And y'all junkies like that death shit."

I accept his answer as making sense.

"It's more like utterly not caring so dying's okay."

"That's why I don't fuck with that shit," he says.

I look at the JIHAD bricks on the coffee table.

"Do you want any of this furniture? I'm sick of it," I say.

The ex-Ranger's wearing gym shorts and a dress shirt with the buttons done up at the wrists.

"Nobody cares about your track marks."

"I care," he says.

I hold the ex-Ranger's head on my chest and I think please surprise me.

The guy who buys me things sleeps with his back to me. I move close so our backs are touching. I think I'm always close to fucking everything up. I think if I'm actually still the same then I'll just give in. I'll take the money that's on the table.

Morning movies are empty. I get up and climb between the junk-bond guy's knees and sit on his dick. I hold the seat in front of me and watch the screen and after a little while I look over my shoulder to see his complete bliss.

He wasn't really my boyfriend but it depressed me too much to think of it any other way. We had sex in his apartment while the woman he lived with was at work. One day, after three years, she came home early. At that point in my life I had never been more scared. I jerked up the covers to hide my naked body. He sat up and looked over his shoulder with resignation.

"Okay, baby, that's it."

He lived in the projects on Avenue D and like always he had one of the boys who worked for him take me down on the elevator. I was seventeen and this boy was probably twelve.

"What's wrong with you, fancy?" he said.

On my stoop I drink a tall boy and listen to the fireworks on the East River, past Avenue D. They sound small and harmless. The streets are smokeless, lawful. There's nobody setting off anything illegally. There's nobody sitting on the street all day in folding chairs. One day in Dubai I Googled him. He was in federal prison for transporting heroin across state lines. In the mug shot he looked bloated and he had tattoos on his face. I felt that his power over me was gone completely. He was one reason I left New York, like the Sheikh was one reason I left Dubai, but not all the reasons. A man from the building sits down beside me.

"You can see everything from the roof. It's like they're exploding right over your head," he says.

"I like it better down here."

42

I get an actual coconut, with a hole bored through it, and a straw. I must look tropical because on the street even women smile at me. But really I want the meat. I go into the bodega and ask to use their machete.

"No machete," the bodega guy says.

"Come on," I say.

This boat is docked off Tribeca. It's for stationary oyster-eating and martini-drinking in the summer night air. It's sunset.

"You're planning to be a hooker until you die?"

"What's wrong with that?" I say.

I smile at him serenely.

"Well, for one thing the biological fact that no woman over fifty is sexy," the calf's brain guy says.

I flip over a shell on the ice.

"Great, I thought it was forty. More time before I have to kill myself."

He makes an anguished face. I look at the Hudson and feel seasick even though this is a restaurant that does not move.

———

One room is six-foot-tall newsprint photographs of people killing themselves. They're all jumpers. Conceivably some of them are fleeing fire, saving themselves. In all the photos the distance to the ground is cropped out.

"Could you do that?" the art guy says.

"I don't know. Could you?" I say.

We're at the New Museum again. I'm bothering with the art guy again. On the new condition that he pay me at the beginning of a date instead of the end. Because the thought of starting over, of hour after hour in one of those chilly strip clubs, is too much. The art guy knees me so my leg buckles.

"You'd have to push me," he says.

I do everything for the ex-Ranger's dick and it does nothing for me. I sit up on his stomach but my back's still to him. I imagine a still of myself, blown up larger than life, hung on a wall for paying people to see.

"It's the drugs."

"I get it," I say.

He puts his ten fingers on my ass. I jiggle it idly.

At the gym, in the shower, some money falls out of me or off of me. Two quarters swirl around the drain with my hair. I laugh at myself. I walk up naked to the TODAY girl.

"I'm a prostitute. That's what I do."

She looks at me in the locker room mirror. Her expression stays the same.

"I'm an art director," she says.

At the end of a Chinese movie that is otherwise dirtily realistic there is a scene of a man on a tightrope walking fantastically between two buildings. He steps out into the open air and doesn't fall. He is in the background and is not the main thing that is happening, as if there are wonderful things to see if I just shift my focus. I look at my ceiling. *Redemption* is a smug word, I think.

I complain that I'm hungry until the guy who buys me things buys me a Sabrett on the street, outside his office. I look at the street-cart guy. He avoids my eye. He speaks to the guy who buys me things.

"Lucky man," he says.

The guy who buys me things turns his back so that he's blocking him.

"I'm having a hard time getting over this higher offer bullshit," the guy who buys me things says.

I eat the hot dog unhappily.

I look at the junk-bond guy.

"Once when I was a little girl a wild dog chased me all the way down Avenue C."

He smirks.

"You're lying," he says.

"Yes."

I combine our feet on the big bed.

"I love you. Can I say that?" the junk-bond guy says.

"Yes," I say.

It was my first time overseas. I had never before seen real palm trees or the lavender light of the desert and there was something whimsical about it, like an untrue story. The woman who had picked me up at the airport put her hand out. She was wearing a silk headscarf with a gorgeous print and nothing black at all.

"Passport," she said.

I shifted my focus from Dubai rushing past the car's window.

43

"I'm not leaving my wife for you if that's what you're getting at."

He's making me stand on line, outside, in syrupy heat, for spicy chicken sandwiches. I twirl my hair up on top of my head and cock out my elbows and look at the calf's brain guy.

"That's not what I'm getting at," I say.

"It's way more than my interest. Interest rates are shit right now."

"I need air-conditioning."

"Whatever," he says.

The art guy also seems uptight. I think not him, too. The tension is already so high. I slide my hand in his pocket and rub his cock.

"You know you can do whatever you want with me."

"That's not really true," he says.

"No choking, defecating, or death," I say.

"I remember."

I open the art guy's door for the zombie girl.

"Yeah, hey," I say.

———

I have often thought that some beauty brand should formulate a come face mask. The way it dries so fast and tight. I look at the zombie girl sleeping beside me. Right now we could sneak out into the living room, huddle over our phones, and max out all his credit cards. I don't wake her up.

I'm drawn across the Whitney to hundreds of VIA AIR MAIL stickers stuck in red, white, and blue rows. It reminds me of my wall of dope bags as interpreted by the ex-Ranger, because the rows are uneven. From far away it makes a pretty, swirling shape. The Whitney is not where it used to be either.

That night I go to a modern ballet at the Joyce and all the patterns are off-center like a bad print. I don't hate it.

I throw a Cherry Bomb cup at the ex-Ranger's arm and it falls on the floor.

"Right now we could fly to a tropical island and sleep on the beach for three weeks."

The ex-Ranger shakes his head.

"How would we cop down there?" he says.

I sour my lips.

"Since when are you the realist in this relationship?" I say.

"In my head I call you the Sheikh."

The Sheikh laughed as I drew my finger over his princely profile.

"What do you call me?"

"My secret wife," he said.

I blow smoke at the ex-Ranger's closet. He has a hatchet in there, along with all his guns. Those tropical vacations never go as planned.

In the morning he was no longer terrifying, the first man who paid me. He praised me like I had performed well. The cash in the envelope appeared astronomical. I took the elevator to the lobby and the hotel staff weren't frightening anymore either. They all smiled at me. I walked out into Dubai, a gleaming paradise, where everything looked unused, and I never felt so empty.

After he's come but while we're still linked together I start crying. It's silent and if the guy who buys me things can feel the warm tears on his chest he doesn't say anything. I just need a break.

I hold the junk-bond guy's cock between my legs and we softly sway.
    "Amy's going to Africa for three weeks. Stay here with me," he says.
    I open my eyes on his neck.
    "When?"

44

"What pattern do you want?"

I give the nail girl a harsh look.

"That's a weird way of putting it," I say.

I get the rectangles of a crocodile and precisely.

We are in a narrow black box and there is no ventilation.

"You're smothering again."

"Again?" he says.

The calf's brain guy smashes my head into the wall of the bathroom and fucks me that way. I think I don't want to be in this coffin with him.

At PS1 glass marionettes are slaughtering each other. They are re-enacting the Crusades from the Arab perspective.

"Religious art is the worst."

I laugh at the art guy.

"You have a good memory but that's not actually true," I say.

"Do you remember our first date, at my apartment?"

He puts his arms around my neck from behind.

"I knew you were dangerous right away," the art guy says.

I grab his wrists. We are also in a black box but it is big and cooled, with a movie playing on one wall, and it doesn't feel like a coffin at all, just a void. Later I say I feel sick and ask to go home early.

Art is the opposite of life. In life politics is acceptable and religion is not, as a reason to start a war. In Beirut I felt, but did not see, a car explode. In the hotel room the man I was with hugged me close to him. He had brought me on his business trip.

"We are fine," he said.

I remember thinking I could never feel fervor like that and that something was wrong with me.

"Me and my cousin are going to pick up the couch tomorrow or the next day, cool?" the delivery guy says.

"You don't live in the Riis Houses, do you?"

"Fuck no," he says.

He's watching a movie on my computer. I draw my knees up on the black leather couch, which is plain, no design.

"The next day," I say.

I pull three bags out of a bundle and then drop the brick on the floor because the coffee table is gone.

"From JIHAD to XXX."

"Sex sells, too," the delivery guy says.

I agree with him.

The spindly silver stilettos feel like when they break they will also make my ankles shatter. I wear them to the corner.

"It's my birthday, can I get a free pack of cigarettes?"

The bodega guy looks at me.

"Let me see your ID," he says.

"No," I say.

———

It is my birthday. I give myself what I always do.

After midnight I turn on my phone again. I walk thirty blocks to the cop bar.

"Where have you been?" the ex-Ranger says.

I look at him. There's no point.

"Fucking other guys," I say.

He nods at me.

"Right."

"There's no point to you and me."

"Right," he says.

I think he should be like giving my couch away but he's not.

There's a substitute teacher for the stripper class and I'm disgusted. It's not nearly nasty enough. It was already co-opted and now it's naïve, like stripping is a girl-power dreamland. In the steam room a girl who is not the TODAY girl, who acted like a job is a job but probably never wants to see me again after finding out I'm a whore, sighs loudly and repeatedly and I have a strong desire to wrap the cord of a hair dryer around her neck that's probably never been strangled because I am full of fucking rage.

I buy batteries that could be used for my smoke detector. I look at it, disabled, up there on the wall.

I wake up and think I'm not breathing.

"What time is it?"

"It doesn't matter what time it is. I'm paying for the night."

I drop my head back down on the guy who buys me things. It does matter, I think.

If I could see myself with altitude I wouldn't see I'm at a latitude and longitude, on a grid of streets and avenues, a dot among other dots, sometimes still and sometimes scrambling. I wouldn't be able to see myself at all. It matters because time is the one thing I can stop when I decide to. I don't say any of this to the junk-bond guy. I hold the elastic of his boxer shorts in the entrance to his apartment.

"Bye, sweetheart," he says.

"Bye, baby."

I peek over my shoulder before he closes the door.

45

My first pattern, when I was a little girl, was the vinyl floor of our kitchen. It was a red and white checkerboard that gradually crumbled away to show the gritty black tar underneath. My mother never replaced a tile, like she never replaced anything. What was new and shiny got old and fucked-up and stayed that way. She let all things run their natural course and every year the degrading pattern of the kitchen floor made me never want to be anything like her a little more.

I go into Duane Reade purely for the air-conditioning.

"Why don't you guys have café tables so I can eat here?"

The cashier does not want to play this game with me.

"Ma'am," he says.

"Miss," I say.

I hand over the sushi and acetone nail-polish remover for bagging. Even though he called me old I'm in a good mood. The calf's brain guy is on a business trip and I don't have to deal with him this week.

We are skinny-dipping in his pool. It's not late. Sometimes other people come up on the roof but then they go away.

"You're going to get yelled at."

"This is not a co-op," he says.

The art guy twirls my wet hair around his fist.

"When I was a little girl a little boy tried to drown me but I didn't let him," I say.

The art guy pushes my head under the water and holds it there by his cock but not for long. I don't even come up gasping.

The closet is wide open. The ex-Ranger is in a bad mood.

"I brought these back from over there," he says.

He has human fingers in a Ziploc bag on his lap. They are dehydrated and bony. After a long moment I put my hand on his knee.

"I wish I had the first dick I sucked for money. I should have cut it off as a souvenir. I wasn't thinking."

He puts his hand on my knee.

He looks up at me from my pussy and wipes his hand down his naked face. His head is shaved, too. It's new.

"Hooah," I say.

"It's fucking hot," the ex-Ranger says.

I'm adult enough to know that if I painted over the man on my ceiling he would just come back.

In yoga, in the fetal position, I stare at the back of the TODAY girl. In the locker room I feel awkward. I give her the opportunity to ignore me instead of the other way around. She puts her hand around my wrist. I smile. I think I was overthinking. I should ask her to brunch and maybe we can argue about the suicidal poet.

"Hey."

"How much do you cost?" she says.

I give her the lesbian discount. I lace up my running shoes on the couch in her apartment. I was overthinking.

"It's always today."

"It is," the TODAY girl says.

"If you're getting too fucked-up you're supposed to ask the guy for a vodka soda with two straws. That's code so the bartender knows to fill a glass with just seltzer. Strip-club secrets," I say.

The bartender laughs.

"Let me get a vodka soda with one straw," I say.

"Coming up."

The guy who buys me things eats a large handful of peanuts. He speaks to me when the bartender moves away.

"When are you going to disappear for a year? I want to know."

"Not yet. Maybe never," I say.

I fix the junk-bond guy's eyebrows.

"Three weeks is a long time. You're going to get sick of me," I say.

"It's going to be the best vacation I've ever had and I've been to Bora-Bora."

"Ooh."

"Twice," he says.

I give him both dimples.

The gynecologist puts lube on two of her fingers.

"This is my hand," she says.

I feel the surge of affection I always feel for the stranger who notifies me before jamming part of himself or herself inside of me. She feels for my uterus and ovaries and the strings of my IUD. After the little boy tried to drown me and I saved myself, in the public pool on the far side of Peter Cooper Village, my mother apologized to his mother on behalf of me, for crying and making a scene. It reminds me of when I said I was sorry for my own blood on the sidewalk, suddenly.

"Perfect," she says.

46

I smear sour cream on a cheese pierogi.

"I'll probably never go to Poland," I say.

"I hope I never do again."

The blue woman is sitting across the table from me.

"I'm happy you're still alive."

"Either way," she says.

"I have a really nice mattress and box spring. It's from Bloomingdale's. Do you want it or not?"

I go to Sixth Avenue to look for the Polish magazine seller. He's not there. I wanted to buy that magazine from him for two dollars, final offer, and then throw it away. I'm not Polish or Russian or Slavic in any way.

I'm hugging the calf's brain guy.

"Do you do it different for every man or do you always do the same shit?"

He's grabbing one cheek of my ass in one of his hands.

"Different, but just a little bit," I say.

Against my leg I feel his hard dick.

The art guy is finally on his art trip, which was not in a few weeks but a month. Of course he has no regard for my schedule. I don't know what to do with myself. I take the train to Queens.

"It's Tuesday," the ex-Ranger says.

"I know."

As a lover when you don't care everything comes out right. I curl around the ex-Ranger and bury my face in the back of his T-shirt while he jerks off. I press on his perineum and his balls jump in my hand.

"I can't come. My dick's totally numb," he says.

"I don't care," I say.

"I'd like to go over to your apartment. See how you live," the ex-Ranger says.

"No, you wouldn't. I do in-calls there."

Where his leg is touching mine I feel his hurt but only for a second before it's muffled by heroin. I look at his closet from our cocoon on the futon. I think those fingers make everything easier.

"What are you going to do with your arsenal?"

The ex-Ranger's holding his hands up in the air, with his thumbs linked, but he's not looking at them.

"Probably nothing," he says.

He night-sweats and I can't stand it. I imagine him covered head to toe in blood that's not his. I cringe to the far edge of the futon but his arm reaches out and finds me. I let him seep over me.

In the morning I walk on his back. Everywhere it cracks. He's a killer, that's who he is. He's just an echo of the Sheikh, not a new pattern. That's who he is, too.

The ex-Ranger and I sit on a bench in a park in Queens. We aren't bickering. We're in the soft center part and we can't keep our eyes open.

"I do love you," I say.

"I do love you, too," he says.

In the future we don't exist.

He runs his thumb under my crocodile nails.

"You're going to stay tonight, too, and forever," the ex-Ranger says.

With his shaved head I think he looks nothing like the Sheikh or the man who lived in the Riis Houses on Avenue D. We're standing on the street outside the cop bar and he's holding my hand like I'm a lady.

"Baby, you and me are just fantasy," I say.

I go home, even though it's Wednesday night, because I want to sleep on my padded mattress and box spring one last time more than I want to stay with him on his thin futon. Of course I never do in-calls at my apartment. This place is mine.

I leave prints on the office bathroom mirror of the guy who buys me things. I curl my fingers into my palms immediately.

"Where's your Windex?"

He's washing his dick in the sink.

"I have no idea," he says.

The junk-bond guy comes back to our bench with lemon ice but I don't want to eat it.

"Everything I do for you," he says.

"If I don't ask for something I don't want it," I say.

He throws the plastic spoon at the fountain. This is in Manhattan, in Washington Square Park, and we're bickering. In the future we don't exist either. I try to picture the last man who called me by the name I gave the junk-bond guy and I can't.

In Dubai even the Russian girls thought I was Russian. I decided to accept the fake look of my face. I only used Slavic diminutives of my real name so I had to rotate them. There was one I reserved for the men who didn't have to pay—for my boyfriends like the ex-Ranger and for the Sheikh.

47

I wake up burning myself on the floor of my apartment.

"Jesus fuck," I say.

I flick the hot cherry off my leg into the iced-coffee cup I'm using for an ashtray. It fizzles in the black water. Sometimes it's like I've learned nothing in my life.

By the twenty-first course I've run out of shiny conversation. I lay my hand inside of his.

"I wish we didn't have to eat."

"You make me so unhappy. You make me feel worse than 2008," the calf's brain guy says.

I stare at a teaspoon of blinding pink sherbet.

"You haven't punched me in a while," I say.

"What's the point?"

On the art guy's computer screen he's wearing a checkered kaffiyeh.

"One girl's Israeli, the other's Palestinian," he says.

"It's like your cock's the one-state solution."

He laughs giddily. I pull him by the belt to me.

"I make you feel good, not bad, right, baby?"

Now I'm wearing the kaffiyeh. He's wrapped it around my neck.

"Baby, you're all icing," the art guy says.

I throw the scarf over my head to cover my hair.

"Tell me everything about Tel Aviv. How was the Middle East?"

"Fuck my mother," the ex-Ranger says.

"Fuck my mother," I say.

"Fuck my father."

"Fuck my father."

"Fuck my sister."

"I don't have a sister."

We're drinking. I'm sneeringly talking to him like he's one of them, like I'm charging him. That makes everything easier, too. The sun is coming up.

"Fuck you," he says.

"Fuck you," I say.

I text the delivery guy from the futon.

"FUK QUEENS," DG texts.

The wax lady tosses baby powder on my vagina.

"It's good you came today."

"I feel good about it, too," I say.

"I have to go to Brazil tomorrow, my father passed away."

One of her latex hands is on my stomach. I put my hand on top of it and press it to me.

"It's okay," she says.

"I'm trying to picture you in black."

She laughs. She points at the black trash bag I brought her.

"Please, I can't take the clothes. They're too beautiful."

"Why not? They're all white," I say.

I made an Emirati feast using only his hot plate. It took hours. He took the first bite and I was full of apprehension. I put a bite in my mouth, too, but it was like I couldn't taste it until I heard his verdict on a dish he hadn't taught me.

"Baby. Where did you learn to make machboos?"

"From the Internet," I said.

He looked at me skeptically.

"Pretty good. Too much turmeric," the Sheikh said.

He ate it for days until it was finished.

By the register I try on a series of increasingly expensive sunglasses.

"Do I make you unhappy?"

The guy who buys me things doesn't answer me. He turns the price tag dangling delicately by my ear. He speaks to the salesgirl.

"Do these cost the most? The ones she has on? They're the ones she wants. It doesn't matter if she likes them or not."

On Mott Street at a bubble tea café we eat sweet potato fries with sugar on them. I choke on a tapioca ball. It flies up the fat straw straight into my esophagus. Throughout my coughing fit the junk-bond guy has a lack of panic on his face.

"Don't drink so fast," he says.

"I don't care if you're happy," I say.

I can barely talk. I have no air.

"I can't understand anything you're saying," the junk-bond guy says.

Out of all of them I think of him as my last choice.

48

"In one second the sun emits more energy than has ever been made in the entire history of humanity, did you know that?" I say.

The delivery guy looks in my eyes, at my pupils.

"Shit's fire, right?"

We're sitting on the floor. My coffee table is gone and my couch and my mattress and box spring. I have been sleeping on a bed of faux-fur coats.

"When they delivering your new furniture?" the delivery guy says.

"They said fifteen minutes like three days ago."

He laughs. That's what he always texts: "15 MIN." I squeeze his arm. I buy eight bricks and every bag says DONT HURT EM.

"I did that for you special," he says.

I text the calf's brain guy a picture of my fingers entwined on a bed of fake fur with the message, "Do you remember how gushing wet I was when you broke the little one?" He does not reply.

I drag the trash bag I brought with me into the center of the salon.

"For the ladies," I say.

It's my black clothes because I only want to wear red. They open it and squeal. I have made them totally happy. I'm distracted. I look at the nail girl.

"Just do whatever you want," I say.

"Nice nails."

They're 3-D Hello Kitty. I keep glancing at my hands and startling myself. I look at the man in the art guy's kitchen.

"Who are you?" I say.

"Ron. I drive a limousine. Here," he says.

He gives me a business card. I cross my arms and turn to the art guy. He pulls me a little away and whispers in my ear, not bossy though, tentatively.

"Just give him a quick blow job and he'll give us the coke gratis," the art guy says.

I look at him calmly.

"No," I say.

I pick up my purse from the island. All the way out of the apartment, and in the hallway, I brace for a hand to grab me, probably by the hair. In the elevator my heart's still racing. Now he's my least favorite.

In Dubai, when I lost a client, I would go to the Saudi's parties to replace him. They were disgusting, all-night gangbangs. I would look up, or over my shoulder, at a new man's face, feeling a new man's cock in me, and I would smile at him and think, each time, I have never hated any person as much as you.

Our tongues are in each other's mouths and sometimes, after a long time, I move my lips and sometimes, after a long time, he moves his. I keep my hand on the ex-Ranger's pocket so I can feel the ten grand I just gave him. I said, "Money solves most things."

———

There's a small ache in my chest cavity like I could have a heart attack. I get a cheap massage on Thirty-First Street. When the girl gets to my feet she shakes one of them.

"Relax," she says.

I keep checking my phone for the calf's brain guy.

"No phone. Put away."

"Leave me alone," I say.

She's a stranger and I don't like her. She makes me miss the wax lady's gloved hands ripping out my pussy hair.

"Don't worry. No Szechuan today," I say.

Her oiled hands stop on my leg. That's code for a happy ending.

"You a cop?" she says.

The waiter gives me his complicit smile.

"No water for the lady, right?"

"Wrong, I want flat," I say.

When he's across the room, against the wall, I sneer at the waiter and he sneers at me. In here every suit is good. Outside, above Central Park, the sky is corroboratively blue.

"It's amazing nobody blows this place up."

"They think they might get to eat here one day," the guy who buys me things says.

I hold his cock beneath the tablecloth.

"Listen, I'm going away but only for three weeks. I promise. I love you," I say.

I walk across the West Side Highway on the pedestrian bridge. I walk through a mall with a food court that's even more mysteriously suburban than the Time Warner Center. Past that is Goldman Sachs. At the security desk I ask for the office of the calf's brain guy.

"You're not on the visitors list."

"It's a surprise," I say.

I'm wearing my tightest red dress. While the guard makes a call I wait. He smiles at me and I smile at him.

"I'm sorry."

"What?" I say.

The guard shakes his head. I feel my face do something ugly but then I correct it.

"Okay," I say.

I walk around Midtown at lunchtime and it's so packed with tourists I have to go in the street. I walk from Broadway to Park, up a few blocks, and then back again, in the shape of a rectangle. Of course I don't always get what I want.

"Next week," the junk-bond guy says.

Between us in the tight, prewar elevator is the doorman I don't like. He is obvious like that waiter. He judges me like there's morality in the service industry and he's good and I'm bad. But I look at his burgundy back and have a feeling of magnanimity. He does have to wear that stupid hat all day.

"I'm ready," I say.

When the bodega guy pushes six dollars across the counter I push it back to him.

"Keep the change," I say.

I put my right hand over my heart. He does the same. I have always fought it but I am a nice person, I think. I also give him my laptop. Back at my apartment I pack and then I turn around in a circle. I open my closet, which is now mostly empty.

49

The junk-bond guy has a bottle of champagne. I sit down on my knees in front of him.

"Don't you want to shake it up and spew it all over my face like it's your come?" I say.

"I never thought of that," he says.

I put my phone between his feet.

I have never been here at night. The apartment's weird art makes it feel possessed. I stand just in the threshold of the dark living room, staring at it, like anything that bothers me, until either I'm mesmerized or its effect is lost and it becomes like everything else.

In the kitchen we eat the breakfast he's made. I try to match his elation.

"God, it felt so good to sleep with you all night," he says.

"Yes," I say.

"Is that how you like your eggs?"

I look at the yolk running all over my plate, which is exactly what I hate.

"Yes."

At a certain calculated point when I'm sucking the junk-bond guy's dick I open my eyes and look up. I like him just as much as the guy who buys me things, I think. So what if he's retired, what's the difference?

The junk-bond guy comes back too soon from the bathroom and catches me kicking the baby coffin.

"Don't do that," he says.

In the night I can feel he can't sleep so I wiggle down and give him a blow job. Then I lay my head on his belly.

"I wish you were here every night. I'd never have insomnia," he says.

"If you bought me for a year you could have me whenever you wanted," I say.

"How much would that cost?"

His voice vibrates through his skin. He's almost asleep.

"You tell me."

It's morning. I sit beside him on the living room couch with a mug of coffee. I smile at him.

"Domestic."

The junk-bond guy flaps down his newspaper.

"How about a million dollars? And I'd come over to your apartment when I wanted. Or I could rent you one. What do you think?"

"Let me think about it," I say.

The formal dining room is perpetually set. I sit at the head of the table. I nod and am infiltrated by china and crystal patterns of the subtlest kind. They get under my skin and wind. A difference is he offered to pay me more than the guy who buys me things. I think I still have plenty of time to think and I feel sad but only for a second. It's muffled right away. I find the junk-bond guy.

"We should eat in the dining room tonight," I say.

"Anything you want, baby."

I duck under the tablecloth and crawl to his chair while he unzips his pants and takes his dick out. The thought of never thinking again, ultimately, is what made me sad and it surprised me.

The junk-bond guy opens the bathroom door that doesn't lock. He looks at me anxiously.

"Do you want some?"

"No," he says.

He closes the door. I bend over to snort the third of three bags off the counter.

I pick the desk drawers in the maid's room until I find my phone. I don't touch it. I lock it back up.

After lunch the junk-bond guy takes all the place settings and centerpieces off. I climb onto the table so the runner is between my knees. He motions me from his chair. I have never done this where the client and I are only together, all the time. It creates an intensity.

The Qatari man's kandura was shiny and his ghutra was starched in the shape of a cobra. The man who bought my passport back for me from the woman with the silk headscarf was Emirati. His kandura had a long tassel and no collar. I knew the man who tried to kill me was Saudi because his kandura was skintight with French cuffs and gold cuff links. At the hospital the nurse, a woman all in white like a man, did not say, "What happened?" And I did not have to say, "I don't know."

I wake up and turn over and see the junk-bond guy, who is naked beneath the white sheet. The man is the random factor and I'm the fixed. I think today is the ex-Ranger's birthday.

The hall is long, the length of the place. I listen to one of those robot vacuums and then I see it as it passes by the opening to the living room and then I only hear it again. I pull my feet up on the couch and watch the maid. She dusts around me and we don't speak.

"What was that you had the other day? Coke?"
    I almost laugh at the "other day" part of his question but I don't.
    "No," I say.

"All you have to do is say a year from the eighties and my teeth start grinding. In the early nineties it was crack," he says.
    He pulls up his lip to show his gold molars.
    "That's how I got these. But I have twenty years clean."
    We're smoking on the smoking couch. I swing my crossed leg.
    "Do you ever let the maid in the maid's room?" I say.
    The junk-bond guy laughs.
    "No, this is my cave. I like it stale."

I stretch out all four limbs but I still can't feel the edges of the big bed. The junk-bond guy comes back from the bathroom and now it's always too soon.
    "Scoot over," he says.
    I do and my wrist flies into open air.

I play with my hair. Each time I make a higher and higher bouffant. I model them for him.

"You're a woman of many skills."

"Let's go for a walk," I say.

"Why?" he says.

I put my hands on my naked hips. My hair falls down. It was in an impossible position.

In a far corner of the living room, almost hidden, I find one of those African fetish objects that must be menstruated on every month. I stand in front of it so long the junk-bond guy comes up behind me.

"I think that's from Mali."

I lean into him. I make my voice sarcastic like I don't care.

"Does your wife smear her period blood on it every month so it doesn't murder both of you?"

He snorts.

"Amy started going through menopause like three years ago. It's a nightmare. Don't let it ever happen to you," he says.

I glare at it.

"What are you going to do when you can't work anymore? Do you have enough money saved?"

"It's never enough. You know that," I say.

We are at opposite ends of the dining room table, eating one of the heated-up dinners that the maid made. He lifts his wineglass to agree with me.

"I'm going to kill myself," I say.

The junk-bond guy looks at me seriously, through the shedding flowers between us.

"So am I. Eventually Viagra won't work anymore either," he says.

Late at night I have a recurring nightmare, while I'm awake, of my lifeless body, my brain dead, completely undefended from the touch of others, their whims.

In the morning living room we dance. Sun streams in. He turns me. He lifts my arm and I hold his thumb.

"What are you grinning about?"

I shake my head. Whether the universe is a closed system or not, it's just a cord pulled out of a wall, death.

"Nineteen eighty-three," I say.

The junk-bond guy's face does many things. It settles on amused. We're in the white bed and I'm still sitting on his cock.

"Is that the year you were born?"

I should lie, say 1987 or 1988.

"Yes."

"Can I get a taste?" he says.

"It's heroin," I say.

"I deduced that."

I drag my nails lightly down his chest.

Instead of eating we watch a Romanian movie on his computer with an undercurrent of fear. Motivations accumulate almost imperceptibly.

"When's the exorcism?"

"Just wait," I say.

Instead of sleeping we roll around the bed platonically, feeling each other's skin.

"Tell me about yourself."

His pupils are pinned and it makes me feel close to him. I think I should reply the way I always do. I should say what I said after the first time he said that, on our first date.

"Okay," I say.

50

"I've never been to Dubai," the junk-bond guy says.

"It's shopping malls and desert," I say.

"Like Phoenix."

I laugh. He got up to puke twice but we're still in the bed. I've heard the first birds.

"So you're eighteen, you get to Dubai, then what?"

I can't get my wings even. I make the right side thicker to compensate. Then I have to make the left side thicker. It's an endless cycle. I remember the girl who told me about Dubai, in the bathroom of the club where we were bottle girls, saying, "Eyeliner can tell when you're afraid." I throw my liquid-liner pen at the bathroom mirror.

I sit on his lap and he feeds both of us pork lo mein on a plastic fork.

"Did you miss it over there? Bacon? Ham sandwiches?"

"You get over it," I say.

He doesn't want his fortune cookie.

"Why not?" I say.

"I don't believe in them," the junk-bond guy says.

"Of course you don't."

I open both of them. A NICE CAKE IS WAITING FOR YOU. I get that twice.

After dark I go into the far corner of the living room and stare defiantly at the African fetish object. I think I will have my period next week.

"Hands and knees."
There is a lag before I do it. He kicks me in the back of the leg.
"Listen to me."

The junk-bond guy talks to his wife in the maid's room with the door shut and for an hour I can't have a cigarette. I think the other person I have spent this much uninterrupted time with was my mother and that turned out badly.

While I'm fixing my smeared makeup he lingers in the doorway to the bathroom.
"I don't know why you bother. You're not going out," the junk-bond guy says.
I smile to overdraw my lips more precisely.
"It's part of the whole thing," I say.
He stays where he is.
"Do you want more heroin?" I say.
"No, it's fucking with my cock."
I smack my lips together, stop smiling.

"You're not like the other prostitutes I've been with. But I'm sure you hear that all the time."
"I'm exactly like them," I say.
Behind his reading glasses his eyes squint.

I try to follow a drawing that is hung on the living room wall. It is a flowchart of conspiratorial connections of the military-industrial complex. The artist must have found it only logical but its illness is so apparent. I give up. It doesn't bother me at all.

There is no grand pattern. Only the small, negotiable, meaningless patterns I have created that have not kept me safe. I eat my ham sandwich and look at him on the other side of the dining room table.

When the junk-bond guy asked me why I became a whore I thought of my teenage self. I said it was because I liked money. Because it was a simple straight line. It was yes. Now over and over to him in bed I say that.
    "Yes, baby. Yes."

He also asked me what I thought about to stay so wet and to answer him truthfully. I answered the way I always would, with a lie, and I felt like myself because what I think about is mine. In the middle of the night I go to the bathroom and jerk off silently with my forehead pressed to the closed door. I feel my whole life since I was twelve years old ooze over my fingers.

At the dining room table I sit where I can watch the back of the maid in the kitchen while she does our dishes. I cross my high-heeled sandals up on an opposite chair.

I look contemptuously at my Hello Kitty nails on the junk-bond guy's dick. Afterward he's helpful and brings me a wet washcloth to get the come off my top.

"What's with all the red?"

"I want to look like a woman and not a little girl."

I retie the bow beneath my tits.

"What?" I say.

He shakes his head, stops smirking.

"Yes. We were together for seven years."

I take the last bite of our bar of ice cream. I pull the wooden stick through my teeth.

"This man you loved, who didn't care you were a prostitute, what did he do for a living?" the junk-bond guy says.

"He made bombs," I say.

In the dark the junk-bond guy traces the shape of my face. It's relaxing. I close my eyes.

"So do you know how to make a bomb, after seven years?" he says.

I'm almost asleep.

"In theory."

Once I asked the Sheikh, "Do women make bombs, too?"

"Everything's possible," the Sheikh said.

Then he laughed. He did care that I was a prostitute.

In the maid's room the junk-bond guy holds up his cigarette.

"Has a client ever burned you?"

"Of course," I say.

"I would never do that."

I don't say it doesn't matter. Or that in a way I prefer it because it's a simple straight line.

"I know, you're nice to me."

The bath is as oversized as the bed and we both fit. I arch my back against the faucet. I put my soapy feet up on his shoulders. I wiggle one of his ears with one of my toes.

"Are you sick of me yet?" I say.

"Not yet."

I squint at him. He's not a stupid man. Maybe he's less stupid than all of them, even the calf's brain guy.

"All day I try to think of new ways to please you."

He grabs my foot and kisses its sole.

"You're everything good, baby," he says.

"Decay," the junk-bond guy says.

The hairs that are gray on his chest feel like wire. They are even deader than regular hair, like dead is a phased state. I think the suicidal poet would like that. I spin one around my finger. I think the secret to a successful suicide is irreversible momentum.

"New things are dumb," I say.

I let up on the tension and the hair slackly spins the other way.

I scowl into the open refrigerator.

"You can put whatever you want on the grocery list. You can even cook me dinner," the junk-bond guy says.

He's standing right beside me. I have no room to maneuver. I grab the cheese.

"I don't cook," I say.

My clothes are the same shade of red as the baby coffin, not the two-man saw over the mantel. It's a true, bright red. I don't think I would fit in there, much less him and me. While I'm nodding the baby coffin, a shoe, grows true-red laces that furl to the floor. It is not unpleasant. I look at him on the living-room couch beside me.

"Why don't we walk over to your office? We could have lunch at that diner, get a couple of those good martinis."

"We're not going anywhere," the junk-bond guy says.

"You said you were going to ask me something later. Remember? A long time ago when we were talking about where we went to high school. We made a deal."

He pours more wine in my glass.

"You answered already. I didn't even have to ask," I say.

I watch him search his brain. He doesn't find it.

"What was it?" he says.

"If you don't know I'm not telling."

I pour more wine in his glass.

The junk-bond guy's reading in bed and I'm lying there on my stomach. He lowers his book. He squeezes the hand on my ass.

"What was it?"

I shake my head. In a few seconds he starts reading again.

"I'm going to give you a stock tip, for the future," he says.

"An insider stock tip?"

"Don't call it that."

I go into his son's room and drag out boxes until there is room enough to sit in the closet and then I close the door. The junk-bond guy opens it.

"What are you doing?"

"Please, I want to be alone for one hour," I say.

He closes the door. I feel strange. Like maybe I am unraveling. I think in the future there is no nice cake waiting for me.

In the sideboard mirror he watches himself fuck me. I lay my face on the runner. We're both on top of the dining room table and I'm sure it will break. It doesn't. What I wanted to know that I didn't have to ask was how much he got for his bonus.

"Why did you come back here?"
   "What?"
   I float in the bathtub with my hair spread out around me.
   "To New York," the junk-bond guy says.

I fall asleep with his hand over my mouth.

51

An astronomical X-ray of the ultraluminous type exceeds the possibility of luminosity. It is a disk of matter accreting, radiating as it's sucked into a black hole. It reveals the universe for what it is, which is being ripped apart. I listened to what he was telling me.

"Like me," I said.

"What?" the Sheikh said.

I grinned at him.

"Ultraluminous."

"Yes."

I get into yoga poses for him. I let my knees fall down by my ears and look up at him standing over me.

"Why didn't you go to the police? He's just going to do it to another woman," the junk-bond guy says.

I told him I came back to New York because of the man who tried to kill me.

"You don't know what you're talking about. I was a whore in a Muslim country. There was no police for me," I say.

I eat a peach at the kitchen sink and look out at the empty courtyard. The junk-bond guy comes by and throws something at my back.

"Don't stand in the window."

"There's nobody out there," I say.

Rich people are never home and the doormen already know everything or think they do. I pick up the pack of cigarettes and follow him into the maid's room.

"Your mother must have thought you would go to college. After going to all that trouble of getting you a scholarship to Sacred Heart."

"She thought I would meet a man who would marry me and take care of me for the rest of my life."

"So you said fuck her," he says.

We are looking at each other, turned on our sides, in the bed.

"In a way," I say.

The junk-bond guy hands me a section of the newspaper and makes his face upset. I look at the headline. It's about Krakow, Poland.

"These terrorist attacks are terrible," he says.

"Terrible things happen every day, just not to you," I say.

"Do terrible things happen to you every day?"

"Not every day. I've been lucky for a prostitute."

The junk-bond guy butters half an English muffin and gives it to me.

At four o'clock we watch the market report and I curl up beside him and lay my head on his chest as he explains things to me.

"Are you paying attention?"

"Yes," I say.

I am. I cup his balls in my hand.

"Do you prefer high-yield bond?" I say.

"That's what they're called," the junk-bond guy says.

I don't change his name in my head.

He licks my clit again and I come again. Heroin is an echo but an orgasm is a pattern. It is the same tiny escape each time, never less. I think of the ex-Ranger. I think of every man I have ever picked for myself and the pattern they've made. The Sheikh was different and not because I loved him more.

After the man tried to kill me I swore off all patterns as ritual, superstition. In a few days they came back. I know I didn't kill the man who tried to kill me because then I would have heard from the police or the Saudi or the Sheikh. I go to the bathroom and then I stay. I lie down. I should have brought a pillow. Eventually the junk-bond guy finds me.

"Can't sleep?" he says.

"Is this what it's like to be married and never be alone?"

He sits down on the floor beside me.

"No," he says.

"You're the best fuck in the world."

The junk-bond guy tucks my hair behind my ear. I take it out.

"I've worked hard," I say.

"It seems natural," he says.

I say what I've prepared in my head.

"If we could see what was coming we would kill ourselves. Blindness is what keeps us alive."

He nods at me. I get up from the living room couch even though I just sat down.

"I need coffee," I say.

I inch into a stinging bath. He opens the door I just shut.

"I'm worried that you're planning something," he says.

"What?" I say.

"To kill yourself."

The bath stops hurting and becomes a warm embrace.

Across the dining room table I smile at him.

"Are you sure you didn't want to go out? After dinner we could have walked along the river."

"I'm fine, baby," I say.

In the master bedroom I hug him close to me. Outside there's no car bomb. There's no sound at all coming up from nighttime Sutton Place.

"We are fine," I say.

The junk-bond guy moves down. He traces the scars on my thigh with his finger and then his tongue.

The junk-bond guy is adding to the grocery list. I tell him I want a sheet cake.

"Like with a design? Like HAPPY BIRTHDAY?"

"Whatever they have premade. A party cake," I say.

He writes it down.

"What I really want is sushi from Duane Reade," I say.

"They have sushi at Duane Reade?" he says.

I sit on the dresser while the maid remakes the bed with big white sheets.

"Before you would've had to live here," I say.

"No, no," she says.

When she brought back the groceries she set the cake and the Duane Reade bag apart from the rest. She turns away from me. She won't be back again before I leave. I know her schedule now.

———

We have spicy tuna rolls for dinner. The junk-bond guy puts a piece in his mouth cautiously.

"This is maybe dangerous."

"Stop being so bougie," I say.

I can't eat mine either.

"Can I serve you a piece of cake?" I say.

The cake is white with two fat blue roses and it says nothing. The junk-bond guy holds up a withered piece of ginger.

"I don't think you're really okay," he says.

I take my phone out of the desk drawer and make a call. It is three in the morning. At the click of the connection I feel panic that is hot and cold at the same time. I squat to my feet to keep from blacking out. She picks up on the third ring. I don't say anything.

"Baby. Are you okay?" my mother says.

I hang up.

I tap out another bag. I just snorted three. I've never done four bags at once before. I've never been over nine bags a day. I could run out or not wake up.

"Fuck."

I scrape it back into the DONT HURT EM glassine.

"It's Friday. It's our last weekend together."

He drops his head on the nape of my neck.

"We made it," I say.

He just fucked me up against the apartment's front door and my face is still smashed to it. I look out the peephole at the empty hall.

I rise up on my forearms and look at him.

"This is the sphinx pose."

The junk-bond guy turns a page in his book.

"You did choose this. Sex work. Nobody forced you."

"I did choose."

I lower back down onto my stomach.

"It doesn't change what it's done to me," I say.

I wait with my forehead to the bed. It takes too long for him to turn the next page.

I'm bleeding and I get some of it on two of my fingers. I walk from the bathroom to the living room and wipe my fingers over the humped back of the African fetish object and then I walk to the bedroom and lie down again.

On TV it is the anniversary of 9/11.

"Where were you?"

"I don't remember," I say.

The junk-bond guy laughs. I don't ask him where he was. He tells me anyway.

I was in Dubai. I had been there two weeks and whoring was still a new thing. Sometimes I told those first men I was from New York and usually they said, "I'm sorry for you. But in most places terrible things like this happen every day," followed by one of many musical Arabic phrases that ended in "Allah." In the bathroom mirror I look at my beautiful face that I have always let take care of me.

At the dining room table I sit beside the junk-bond guy and not at the far end.

"What do you think about my offer, for one year and an apartment?"

"Can I tell you next week?" I say.

Underneath, my feet are crossed at the ankle and squeezed between his. I try to put a whole rose in my mouth but it won't fit. His face doesn't look the way I think it should.

"How could you love a man who made bombs that killed innocent people?" the junk-bond guy says.

I bite through the icing and my teeth sting.

"Who's innocent? Everyone is participating from the moment they're born. There's no victims, there's no luck. Don't you agree, Mr. High-Yield Bond?"

"No."

I shrug.

"Love is irrational," I say.

He pushes his plate away untouched.

"Too sweet," he says.

"That gun's still in your purse."

"I told you about that months ago. Why are you going through my things?" I say.

"Why did you bring it here when you knew you were only going to be with me?"

Jesus, I think.

"Because you can never really know anybody."

The junk-bond guy's face is suspicious. He stares deep into my eyes, looking for something. He shakes his head.

"You're so high," he says.

He turns over in the bed so his back's to me.

Before the Sheikh left to slaughter his cow he told me he was going to give me something.

"Here," the Sheikh said.

He was different not because I loved him more but because he taught me something. I wake up in the morning and the junk-bond guy's not there.

————

It's been too claustrophobic. I've said too much. I say my name in the bathroom mirror.

"It's going to be okay," I say.

I walk by the living room.

"Let's smoke a cigarette," I say.

He's sitting on the living room couch with his arms crossed, not reading the newspaper, not doing anything. I go into the maid's room to wait for him. I think maybe he won't come but he does. He sits down on the couch beside me and I stand up. My purse is by my feet. I brought it with me secretly. He didn't notice or he wouldn't be here. I steel myself. I point the ex-Ranger's gun at him. I see on his face what that man who tried to kill me must have seen on mine. It's not surprise. It's terror. It's the most fucked-up thing I've ever seen.

"Please. Have mercy," he says.

The second I know I won't do it I do. I shoot the junk-bond guy twice, in the chest and the head. With the silencer it is silent enough. His legs tremor and stop. I touch him and the life is gone. I recognize it instinctively and know it's the first time I've felt it, death. That's it. I feel crazy with a calm center. From the kitchen I take the slice of sheet cake with the other rose on it that he wouldn't eat and stuff it in what's left of his mouth because one of those fortune cookies was his. I unlock my phone from the drawer. I lock him in the maid's room.

In the elevator I stare at the doorman's back. I think this is a mess. Maybe I overreacted. Maybe he didn't know. It's still Sunday. It's not even next week yet. But now it's started and it's irreversible.

"How is it outside?"

My voice sounds elated. The doorman makes an okay sign with two fingers.

From the time I returned to New York I have given myself fifty-two weeks, one year.

52

"Okay, one year. I accept your offer," I text CBG and GBT.

No man dumped me there to die of exposure and dehydration. I drove into the Arabian Desert by myself and then I drove out again. I was there to practice. The air smacked and behind me a wave of sand billowed into a burning cloud. I held the scarf to my head and both crouched and ran. It was five pounds of C-4 explosive, what the Sheikh gave me.

I sit in the middle of a bed at the Pierre completely naked. The calf's brain guy sits on the edge. He's taking off his shoes. I think it will be easier the second time. I wait for him to turn around because I want him to know me, finally. When he does and he sees the gun he has the same look as the junk-bond guy and it's still terrible but a little less this time. He lunges for me and I shoot immediately. I shoot three times. He splatters all over me. I push with both hands and he falls off the side of the bed onto the carpet. I'm crying, I think. I only know because I can feel the tears on my face but then I think maybe that's the calf's brain guy's hot blood. What I wanted was Goldman Sachs. In a frenzy I kick him under the bed.

In his glass bedroom the art guy has blackout curtains. I pull them.

"I thought you were never coming back. That was so stupid, that thing about the coke. I'm sorry."

"This is not about that. This is because you grabbed my arm at a strip club and then when I asked you what you did you said you worked at a hedge fund."

"What?" he says.

As soon as he sees the gun he turns around and runs. I have to chase him. I have to shoot him in the back four times. He falls onto his glossy kitchen floor and I slip and fall down beside him. He's so heavy. He's two of me, like all of them. I drag him by the wrists, gasping and sweating and crying again, definitely this time and uncontrollably, back into the blacked-out bedroom. I lock the door. I give myself a whore's bath in his bathroom sink. I try to compose myself. I wipe off my makeup and do it all over again. The eyeliner can't tell but I'm afraid. My wings come out exact, even. I unzip the garment bag I've brought. I put on a bright red, skintight suit. Off the art guy's island I snort another bag. I want to be certain my face will look the way it always does. In the living room I turn on his camera on its tripod and sit down on his couch. I cross my legs and then I cross my arms on top of my knee so my wrists and hands dangle delicately in the air. I see myself in the viewfinder. My face is seductive. I look into the recording eye of the camera silently. After five minutes I stand up and walk out of the apartment. I leave the video running.

On my phone almost all my voice mails are from the ex-Ranger. I listen to the last one.

"Katya. You whore," he says.

On a street in Queens I stand across from his apartment. What I would like is to have sex with him and while he's fucking me to look at him above me and will him to open his eyes and see me so I could tell him it was the last time and it was with him. Then I might kill him, too. I might unlock his closet and get out the hatchet he has in there and hack off his fingers on both hands, not just one. I text him.

"Check your mailbox, baby. I just gave you something."

I walk back to the train. He can stay alive in the dying universe somewhere like the Sheikh, as an echo of the Sheikh. What I gave the ex-Ranger was all my money. I throw my phone in the trash.

My apartment smells stale. The sponge on my kitchen sink is shriveled and stiff. I open my closet and on its floor is a tarp. I lift up the bomb I've made and put it gently in the box for the pressure cooker and then I put the box in a big Barneys shopping bag. I find blood behind my ear and I don't know whose it is, like it's come. I laugh. I think maybe it's for the last time. When I look out the window the two razed lots are geometrical with steel girders and now I can't see where I used to live. I say something to the city even though it can't hear.

I carry the shopping bag in my arms, against my tits.

"What's that?" the guy who buys me things says.

"A pressure cooker."

I set it down on one of the chairs in front of his desk and then I wander into his bathroom. I sit on the bathroom counter. I unbutton the one button of my red suit jacket. Underneath I'm naked.

"Fuck me," I say.

He fights me when he sees the gun. He slams my wrist into the bathroom wall. We struggle. We roll all over the cold tile floor. I have eight bullets left but it's the middle of a workday. He's bigger than me. He's stronger. I'm lucky. I stab him in the balls with the point of one of my heels. He yells but we've had sex in here so many times. I get the gun flush to his neck, behind his ear, and shoot once. For a few seconds I'm unmoving, holding the guy who buys me things under the armpit, with the bloody Glock in my mouth. I wait. Nobody comes. I snort the last of my heroin. I squat to my feet but tell myself to stand up. From the chair I pick up the shopping bag. I walk out of his office and down the hall. I walk to the middle of the wealth-management floor of Deutsche

Bank. Bankers look at me and I look at them. I think I'm sorry but I can't just shoot the men because then it would only be a domestic dispute between a whore and her clients. I think terrible things happen every day and today it's to you. I put down the bag and open the box. Before there is the suck of pressure, before I change state into light and then ash, I run my hands over my hips, this body. I have no expression on my face. I say nothing. With my foot I kick the switch that is the detonator. I see the world clearly.

ACKNOWLEDGMENTS

Thank you, Sean McDonald, Emily Bell, Chris Parris-Lamb, Maya Binyam, Claude Faw and all of my family, and Richard Hell.

CPSIA information can be obtained
at www.ICGtesting.com
Printed in the USA
LVHW092024211218
601380LV00004B/306/P

9 781250 192738